MW01680181

Copyright - Buried Lies - Deceit Trilogy

Octavia C. Penn

To all who thought they were alone. You are not. You just haven't been in the right place at the right time. The right people will come along and they will choose to stay no matter the darkness you face.

Octavia C. Penn

Buried Lies

BY

OCTAVIA C. PENN

Octavia C. Penn

TABLE OF CONTENTS

Octavia C. Penn

Octavia C. Penn

Prologue

The city is quiet tonight, with only the sounds that are of the rail cars running downtown next to the medical plaza. Hearing people's low whispers as they pass by me while I stand outside of the hospital trying to put together a plan for my future. It is frigid out and in the middle of winter in Fallen, Chicago. This morning when I woke up there was a cast of ice on the surface of everything. While, just under that surface of ice is the soft pillow like snow that I know will be a dingy gray slush by tomorrow afternoon. The weather here changes so drastically no one can keep up. Most of us just ignore the weather just to survive the workday. It is a vicious cycle of hazardous conditions, causing us to stay inside, away from the misery.

The rain drizzles on top of me, giving my brain the forethought that if I want to survive the night, I better get out of this weather. Knowing that I have a price on my head and that someone is looking for me. I quickly head to a little cafe down the street but first to the payphone booth.

The Cafe, is the usual spot we frequent when the clubhouse isn't an option. *"And right now, it isn't an option."* Grabbing the phone, I call my newly acquainted friend Richard to have him meet me at the coffee shop just around the corner. The phone rings and a tired voice answers.

"I need you to meet me asap. This is a matter of life or death!" Knowing sometimes that I can be dramatic, especially with the life we are a part of, Richard scoffed. *"Really.. Which life yours', or mine?"*

"Cafe now!" is all I belted out.

With a quick response from Richard and an even faster hang up on the payphone, I go in and wait in the cafe for him to arrive. Sitting in the normal corner booth and watching all the people pass by outside braving the blizzard, the server comes up, clears her throat and asks me for my order.

"What can I get ya, Hun?"

"*Black coffee, two sugars and one cream...*" I pause for my thoughts, and ask her to *"add a piece of buttermilk pie, please."*

"*Is that all?*" I nod yes and she turns to leave.

About a half an hour goes by, and It doesn't take Richard long to come waltzing in out of the sleet and snow that is rapidly taking over the town tonight. You can hear the wind whip past the buildings as he enters the Cafe and shakes off the weather. Richard, pauses to take his hat and coat off at the door, and hangs it on one of the empty hooks. Richard's demeanor as he looks for me seems tense with aggravation when his eyes stop dead on me. He heads down the aisle of tables and chairs that ends with him sliding into the opposite side of the booth from

me. Placing his hands on the table, he directs his eyes at me and lets out a disgruntled huff.

"Well, what is the life and death situation that you drug me out of my home in the middle of the night tending to

my sick wife for?" Richard grunts in a sarcastic tone. *"You know Prudence is not doing well with her treatments and I need to be home!"* A.J. watching as my head shakes and nods in disapproval of his conscious decisions.

A.J. whispers, "I have a price on my head and I don't know a way out that won't have me killed or not go to hell for what I am going to do?" With such a vague sentence, I roll my eyes at AJ almost getting up to leave him to his maker. Instead I decided to just get direct with him.

Instead I just get direct with him. *"AJ, cut the chit chat shit and just tell me what is going on. Don't lie to me just to get me to agree with you. Then drag me into something that would get me killed as well. That wouldn't be fair to either of our families. Now would it?"* Not sure he heard me, as he seems to be mentally somewhere else, I wait for his response.

"I skimmed some money off the top of some deals to help pay the bills with some of the club's investments. They found out and now I am being hunted down to pay them back with interest and I don't have it. Fortunately they gave me a deal. I have till the end of the month to give it all back or I am dead." AJ's face fades to a pale shade of white and the sweat is building on his face like he just ran a marathon in this

weather. You can tell he is in a frantic manic state and is grasping at straws to figure a way out of this.

"Well, what is your plan... or should I say plans at this point?"

The look on AJ's face tells me this will not end well and I am not sure I want anything to do with it. But he is a friend and we are new to this town, so I need to help for now.

AJ begins to tell me his devious plan to get this money back, and he is right when he says it's something that if he survives, he will end up in hell for.

"I have this plan to switch mine and Jessica's baby on the black market for the money owed to the client," With a shaky voice AJ whispers. His whole demeanor is now in defense mode.

"How could you?

How could you do that to a woman you supposedly love?"

Still waiting for A.J. to show some type of emotion I just let in on him to try and convince him this will be the end of him.

"Knowing that, that is your flesh and blood, you're just so willing to give the baby away as if it never existed?"

A.J. opens his mouth like he was going to say something but then stops himself.

"No forethought on what this will do to Jessica? She has carried this child for nine months. Grown to love her and you're just so willing to throw it all away?"

"Jessica will kill you if she ever finds out what you are up to beforehand."

"That's why she will never know." AJ interjects.

"Let me just tell you, you are delusional if you think this won't come back to haunt you or bite you in the ass!"

He continues to tell me what he wants to do and my mind wonders about my personal problems. Here we are trying our damndest to have a family and he is just willing to get rid of his.

My wife Prudence and I have been trying to have a child of our own, and with her cancer treatments, she has been unable to carry. Trying to rationalize with myself, I cut him off. *"How much do you owe AJ?"* AJ looks at me with a blank stare and I lean in closer to repeat myself again in a lower tone. *"What do you owe the client so they let you go?"*

AJ leans in just as close as he can and tells me *"A hundred thousand dollars."*

"What!" Saying it so loudly I startle even myself and I turn to catch gimps of the cafe we are in and not one person looked up besides the server and AJ just waives her off.

I get up and tell AJ to *"Give me an hour and I'll be back." Disgusted with him but, trying to find an ounce of remorse for the whole situation I get up and leave to give myself some time to take in the information and to get some air. It was getting increasingly stuffy in there as the information just so happened to fall out of A.J's mouth.*

Walking out the door with hat and coat in tow, I head to the payphone booth. Stepping inside, I place the quarter in and dial the home number. Two rings and Prudence answers the phone, coughing, and wheezing trying to catch her breath, she replies, *"Hello, this is the Cosa residence. Can I help you?"*

"Prudence, it's me Richard..., I need you to have an open mind and remember that I want to do this for us.. for you. I know how badly you wanted to be a mother and I can give you this and I will, as long as you are okay with it."

I told her everything and like I expected; the phone went silent. *"This is our chance to become parents, Prudence,"* I calmly whisper into the phone. *"We don't have much time. I need to know if taking the money we saved and the money from your parents' inheritance they left you would be okay to save this child?"*

She hesitates for what seemed like an eternity and I slide another quarter into the machine as the recorded voice of a lady on the phone reminds me this is a pay phone. That I am paying for this time just like everything else in this god forsaken world.

"No, I couldn't imagine Jessica having her baby ripped from her and deceitfully told that it dies just to help what sounds to be a crappy person to call a friend. I knew he was a piece of shit. How could I look her in the face every day of our lives and lie to her? That her child would be right in front of her and not say a word. I am someone who has had miscarriages and suffered that loss and overwhelming pain of losing a child. I couldn't do it to another mother."

Sobs begin to fill the silence on the other end of the line. You can hear the hurt in her whimpers.

"It's a girl." I say with hesitation.

Octavia C. Penn

"Richard, if you feel you need to help him, then make sure the child goes to a loving family. And if he actually does this, then he doesn't deserve the child to begin with. What are you going to do about Jessica when she finds out?"

"Nevermind I don't want to know anything, I want no part of it. Complete deniability of where the child ends up."

"We will cross that road when we get there," with an unsteady voice. Prudence just responds with, *"Stay safe and come home. I need you here with me like you promised until my time comes. You stay safe."*

"I need to take care of something with AJ and I will be right there." pausing for an; I love you, but the phone just rings with a dial tone in my ear. I hang the phone up and head back into the diner when I see AJ in the window cornered by their thugs that have him pinned in a fight mode. *Well, at least he wasn't lying to me. This will make the decision that much easier.* Hoping no one could hear my inner thoughts because I would beat my own ass for this situation.

Walking into the cafe, I make myself quiet and slip up on the big guy standing with his back against me and put my pistol to his head. *"I don't know what you are thinking coming in here and thinking you would get him all to yourself, but if you don't leave now, you won't leave at all."* I pull the hammer back on the pistol that is held at the base of his skull, pointed at an angle to convince him it will do the most damage when I pull the trigger. He throws both hands up and says, "*Okay, Okay we will leave but this ain't over. My boss says to tell you he will collect the money or a body you choose."*

The Beginning

"Jane, Jane, for the last time, as Cole huffs, *please answer me!"* She turns to see her best friend Cole staring at her from the doorframe of the basement wine cellar.

"What did you say?"

My mind is still on the events that unraveled today in the parking lot of the police station.

Cole repeats, *"Are you okay with the choice you made today? You know the one where you ended one chapter of your life and started on another?"*

Cole is right. For the most part I ended one chapter of my life and started a new one all in the same day.

Octavia C. Penn

But I have been ready for this moment for the past two years and counting. For those last two years, I have been battling a failing marriage to a man that just wasn't able to emotionally satisfy me. As I stare back at Cole for what seemed to be forever, it dawns on me that he's still waiting for a response. *"Yes, I'm sure. I'm sure that today will be one of my first steps forward and two steps back in a long line of decisions for my future."*

"Red! Cole shouts out loud with a smirk on his face. We're going to need it after the day you have had."

"I swear if he wasn't so much like my brother, people would think there was something going on between the two of us." When in all actuality he is more like the brother that I never got the chance to have. He always seems to know exactly what to say or do. Showing up exactly when I need him too, being a sense of family that I desperately needed.

Don't get me wrong, my ex-husband isn't a bad man. He supported me in every endeavor that I pursued in my life with gusto. The both of us have always had the notion that if we wanted to do something to always take the initiative to go after it. To never waste a moment in this life because we don't get a second one for a do over. Him pursuing a law degree to being a lawyer and me always wanting a life of uncertainty and feeding that by being a detective on the force made for an interesting talk after long days.

When my marriage felt more like a friendship than a supporting, loving and romantic husband and wife commitment, that's when I knew it was over. Fighting for it for two long years drained me emotionally. We would talk about how we were feeling and for a few weeks it would be good, but then it was back to business as usual. Being married for the past five years slowed time down and I could see us fall apart. It was almost like watching a really long train wreck. So much so I don't know if I can ever muster the energy or emotion to try for another situationship in the near future.

Unless the right one comes along and sweeps me off my feet in the *"Red Room"* manner kind of way, I'm not sure I would want it. *Oh well, I need the time to work on myself and my career. Today in that courtroom was a reminder of just that. Besides, the man I would only consider for that spot in my life at this time is currently not available because he is my boss.*

Cole cranks up the music and adjusts the light for the current mood and dances me around the kitchen. He knows just how to make light of a mood and make me forget my woes. Two bottles of red wine followed by a pitcher of margaritas and time quickly eases into the early morning hours. I couldn't remember the last time I laughed and enjoyed just being me.

Calling it a day, I head upstairs and get ready for bed. As for this day, I am done with it. Soft sheets, heavy comforters and all the pillows in the world take me in as I melt into them for the night.

Thoughts in my head about *"I need more 'girlfriends' because there are three men in my life that keep things kind of in an array state of chaos."* The friend, the boss, and the ex. Which I have recently kicked to the curb through no fault of his or mine. Just life sucks sometimes.

Drifting off to sleep, I leave myself running through memories of that one evening last year when I stayed late to work on an assignment and no one was there besides me, or at least I thought. I heard the copy machine going off and someone beating on it from down the hall and a voice that screamed out, *"you piece of shit!"* With that notion, I got up from my desk to do what I do best and investigate the ruckus. Walking down the dimly lit hallway to enter the room, I see Bryce standing there next to the machine with a bewildered look upon his face. That is when I give a short knock and his face

darts to mine. He responds with, *"I thought I was the only one left here."*

I kind of smirked with a cocky response. *"Nope, my boss is an ass and has me on a deadline, so I have to be here to meet it."*

"Is that so?" Bryce barked back in a snippy manner.

"I would ask what you were doing beating on the copy machine, but I take it you don't know how it works."

"Not really this is something Blake would do but she isn't here."

"Well, let me help you," leaning in and noticing that it's jammed, I slowly squat down right in front of Bryce, leaving me in eyeshot of his lower body. Seeing just how well put together he is makes my body tighten just that much more.

Not that I already clinched every muscle to make myself appear like I can gracefully get down on the floor after being here and working a fourteen hour shift.

Reaching between his legs to unplug the power cord but it makes out to be pinned between the copier and the wall, leaving just enough room not to squish it, still having to give it a yank, and with that it throws me off balance. *"There now you can pull the copy paper out of the rollers, and when you turn it back on, it will reset itself."*

When I tried to get back up, I stumbled forward. Grabbing the inside of his thigh with one hand to keep from falling, he caught me. With one arm around my wrist and the other hand gathering around my waist as he pulls me up within kissing distance to his face. *"There now "* he growls. His words almost take my breath away when he takes a deep breath so close to my mouth. My eyes narrow in on his lips as he purses them together to swallow hard. Bryce's lips are plump and the stubble around them seems like they would tickle if we were to actually kiss. A slight scar shows in the edge of his hairline around his mouth that is hidden unless you get close enough to see it. *In this moment I could see all the imperfections that make him so attractive*. The pause is almost overwhelmed with what tension I felt, so I attempted to step back; he continued to hold me close, not allowing me to budge. But by the look on my face, I guess he noticed when I placed my hand on his that it was firmly wrapped around the small of my back. He quickly let go seeing what position we were in and it made him blush

in the face as he apologized. I smiled and said *"no problem, thanks for the save."*

Thinking to myself, *Really, out of all the things I could have said, I say thanks for the save?* When in actuality I wanted him to take me right there in the room on the copy machine himself.

I turned, trying to leave the room with some grace intact as I headed down the narrow hall to my office. I closed the door behind me, trying to be quiet so he doesn't hear the giddy school girl slump up against the door and slide to the floor. Sitting there in the dark with only a lamp to light my office, I feel my face radiating heat as I am sure it is flushed as well if I only had a mirror to confirm. I remember daydreaming about this man for the rest of the night. Wondering *"Where that moment could have ended up."* Also, being in a marriage like mine is quite lonely, but nonetheless I am married, and wishful dreaming is all that I could have allowed for the moment.

Something seems to be screaming in the background of the room I'm in and at first, I believed that it was part of my dream and I couldn't put two and two together to get out of my own head then I quickly realized that it's six in the morning with my alarm going off *"I needed to get up."*

Rolling out of the bed and dreading the day because for the first time in a long time it's just my decisions, *"Not sure I know how to do that just yet."* The day seems to go accordingly as I make my breakfast and pour myself a cup of coffee, and dance to a bit of old-time rock classics in my kitchen.

Just as I seem to let loose and enjoy the thoughts of being able to do as I please in my own house, I get an odd racket from the upstairs guest bedroom. I had completely forgotten that Cole had slept here last night after our red wine party seemed to have no end.

Cole made his way down, staggering around, and leaning on the banister of the stairs to help aid him against the devastatingly bright light in which gravity has already manipulated his consequences for last night's actions, barely making it to the kitchen.

"How do you feel this morning? Is it the hair of the dog or water and Tylenol that will get you through the next few hours?"

Looking at me like a lost puppy in a cold storm or hell in which he created, he quietly repeated, *"Tylenol and water, please."*

"What's on the agenda for today? I assume your father will be here to pick you up for that important meeting you were telling me about the other day?"

Cole doesn't respond. Instead, he stares at the countertop and his mind drifts to another place.

"Cole, hello Cole. Earth to Mars," Snapping my fingers in his face, forcing him to blink and come back to reality.

Cole looked at me with a smile on his face and replied, "*Richard would not be picking me up here. That I would just be going straight to the office, I would meet him there. No need to stay and babysit the children, so to speak. I won't be here long. I have too much to do."*

Cole's dad is a stockbroker that is about to retire from the walls of Wall Street after being there for thirty years. Among his other after hours shady deals, he commits for the income he makes. We all have an unspoken word that his businesses are off limits to our conversations. It's just better that way. He tells us all that it's time for him to sit on the sands of the most beautiful beaches that he can find and drink in the riches of the day till his heart's content. I don't understand why he hasn't already done so for his son's sake. I mean, when he gets caught, Cole is going to have to figure out a way around all the media and questions concerning his father.

Richard has been raising Cole alone for most of his life when his wife passed away just six months after giving birth from stomach cancer. Richard seems to do a great job with Cole on his own, as I kinda see him as a brother of sorts. We have been friends for the last eight years. We have been inseparable, despite our wins and losses of life.

Cole gets ready to leave, and we say our goodbyes as we chock up last night's woes as a chapter in the book of life.

Onto bigger and better things rushing out the door with that grin and messy hair like always in his fast pace of life following in his father's footsteps. Taking a deep breath and sigh, letting go of the past, I look into this home and smile with the thought of *Today is the day I make myself a priority. No more having to*
wait to accomplish things that I wanted or needed to do on my own.

The mornings are my favorite time of day. I can sit in the sunroom off the back of my brownstone and just listen to the silence and piece together the next steps of my day, week, year, hell my whole damn life. Seems like everyone has their life together, and I'm just now making sense of my own. Not quite sure how I feel yet about being alone? I am not sad, mad or angry but maybe at peace and hopeful for my future and what it in-tales.

My life has always been a slow steam ahead uphill both ways in the snow if you, *"Catch my drift."* Pun intended. They adopted me when I was born, but I had a great childhood and I never really seemed to put a thought to where I came from or even if I had siblings. Both parents passed away in a car accident during the winter when they slid across a bridge on black ice and into the harbor during a rainstorm. Thus leaving me their home and a bit of a nest egg that I'm grateful for, for my future security now that my marriage is over. My distant Aunt left to raise me till I was older then up and leaving me as fast as she could when my plans didn't align with hers. she never really was around when I was born so I never expected her to stick around when I was an adult.

Starting this journey off with a clean slate is somewhat freeing. My thoughts and actions are my own and be damned who doesn't like how I pursue them.

The phone rings and I answer it. *"Hello?"* The dark and thirsty voice on the other end of the phone is one that is all too familiar and needs no introduction when he speaks. *This man has the perfect way of getting under my skin in all the wrong ways along with all the right ways. He could convince me to do any job, any day of the week.* His eyes are the perfect shade of baby blue with a hint of gray. *"Just imagining this man does things to me that seem unspeakable in real life, at least if I say it out loud."* Just like
that, our lives are intertwined and I can't help but want more of a situationship, mostly the kind that doesn't require any thought process above the move your leg here kind.

Cole and Richard

"Cole, get your shit together before I come find you!"

Reading the text message from my father in his voice on the lock screen of my phone with my eyes squinted together to focus this vision of last night's merriment bestowed upon me. Imagining the look on my father's face when he sent this message makes me chuckle in the slightest. Richard has never been the type of person to be patient for anything in my life.

I reply with a short message of my own. *"One hour"* Getting out of the guest bed in Jane's upstairs guest room, I notice the faster I move, the faster the room spins, making my head pound like it's about to explode. With the sound of music coming from the kitchen, I'm sure Jane has been awake for some time now. Needing to get myself pulled together enough to make it to the kitchen to grab a drink of water. While standing is proving to be a bigger challenge. Wobbling down the staircase, I finally make it to the kitchen and see Jane dancing away the morning like nothing happened. *How does she do it?* It doesn't seem like she missed a beat from yesterday's debacles. She spins around and catches me staring at her and you can tell I startled her. Her cheeks blush more than usual and she bellows out a high-pitched laugh. Her responses tell me she is in a great mood and ready to move forward with her life on her terms. She seems to move with a lighter gait. Makes me happy to see her so light and full of optimism.

Saying *"Goodbye"* I head out for work. The ride to work takes no time at all. We pass my favorite cafe and local Mexican restaurant Jane and I eat at once a week. With no time to stop for a coffee, we turn the corner and pull up to work. Coming to a stop, I open the door, say "*thank you*", and get out.

Walking up a long flight of stairs to the entrance of what some would call hell on earth. *I fucking hate the stairs today!* Entering the building and making it to the fifth floor where my desk is, the doors open. To me, this is a world of chaos that I get to maneuver. That excites me. Something about all of it gives me a sense of power dealing with the amount of money that I do every day. Walking through the mob of people bumping and shoving each other as they shout numbers and throwing hands in every direction, making sure they are seen and heard to get to my old man. I finally made it through the crowd and sat down at his desk. Richard looks up and gives me a frumpy look and tells me, *"Don't talk, just listen. I need to get Jane to go to lunch with me and get her out of the house this evening."*

He is always so short and to the point with me which has made it to where we were never really close like a father and son should be. Doing my due diligence I nod and give my confirmation that I heard and agreed to what he ordered me to do. I want to ask him why he needed me to do this, but I know better. It's just better to do as I am told. Richard's last words as I leave his desk for mine are *"Meet me at the ClubHouse at eleven o'clock tonight when it's done."* Turning away, he grunts and catches my attention. *"Eleven o'clock, don't forget!"*

"I got it," snapping back at him at the same time I leave, not giving him a second more to boss me around.

Richard's world is complicated to say the least and to disagree or go against his wishes will be something only an idiot would do. Some say his past and present are shady and that he has current dealings and ties with the local mob. Let's just say like father like son. We both are still trying to make it seem like I am not part of the "Club" but with every job that Richard takes, he sucks me in more and more. I can't say too much because the money is nice. Like the last assignment, I was told no questions were to be asked and if I screwed it up, I would be done. Whatever that meant, but I wasn't about to find out, so here I am an errand boy for my father.

Leaving my desk, I make my way down the stairs, trying to figure out what needs to be done in order for me to distract Jane for the time being. Getting close to her over the years didn't start by my dad wanting to manipulate and deceive. I truly wanted to be her friend. Jane was just happy and bubbly and honest, which was something that I truly needed. Life with my family is always a disarray of plots and schemes. It's nice to have something stable in my life.

Jane

Bryce is a middle-aged man with black hair that is slightly peppered gray with that strong but full of wisdom gait about him. He wears his five o'clock shadow all too well. Standing in the window of his office wearing a vest and white button-up shirt with both sleeves rolled up his forearms with a deep dark red tie and polished shoes. Coming from a wealthy family, he tends to prove to himself that in everything he does, he will make it on his own merit. Fifteen years on the force, and he has made the captain of detectives in record time.

"What is so urgent that I am at the office an hour before I should be?" Shutting the door behind me, I can feel the tension in the room. I turn around and meet his eyes as his

response rings in my ears. *"There has been a body found in the living room of a home on 62nd and Kennedy St. this morning. I need you to cover this and Jane, please keep me apprised of all the details."* Staring into his eyes, I wanted to remind him of what just happened to me yesterday. I mean, it is not really his problem why would he care about my personal life, but I did request this time off. Why would I be the one to cover this story when I put in for my vacation that I so desperately needed? So in my attempt I try to spit out the sentence *"Um ... Bryce, my request off for the next two weeks has been made well in advance, and."*

"Jane, I am aware of the request, but this needs your attention, and I expect nothing less than your best. When this is over, you can take all the time off that you need and I will approve it with pay. You have my word."

"I understand that this assignment is major, but maybe you could ask someone else," I insisted.

The look on his face and with his narrowed eyes that say otherwise. Bryce hands me a file and sends me on my way. *"Close the door on your way out, Jane. Have a great day."* Nodding with my response, I turn to leave, but I am still angry, but I can't let him see that though. My job is the only stable constant in my life right now and I don't need to be looking for a reason to not have it. So, shutting my mouth, I close the door and leave quietly.

Standing in front of the door I had just closed, Blake looks up from her desk at me with her beady eyes and glasses. She just shrugs and looks back down at her computer as if she was too deep in her own business to care about the world around her. I take a deep breath and continue into my office to open the file I was just given. Opening the file to two photos stapled to a medical report and the official police report following behind it.

The victim's name is Jessica White. She is about fifty years old and faced down on the floor with bruises around the hands and a gunshot wound to the back of her head and lacerations to her ribs. Photo evidence of the weapons minus the gun that delivered the fatal blow that ended her life. In the report, there is no name of any next of kin listed, except a police report that states that she has lived at the known address for some time now.

The day seems to fly by when I hear a voice bust through my door and this lanky body lands in one of the seats in front of my office desk. He just plops his feet up on my desk like it is something in the norm. *"Cole, get your feet off my desk! You act like you live here!"*

"Well, you would know. I haven't seen one person who is as committed to their job as you are." Cole is right. *"You are supposed to be off. What is going on?"*

"Well, with recent events that landed on Bryce's desk, he thinks I am the person for this job, so now I've got to be here."

With a knock at my door, Bryce stops in to tell me, *"The bank will be at the house to hand over a set of keys for the investigation. Expect to work late tonight. We need to get a lead as fast as we can to get this killer caught."*

Cole whips his head around to give Bryce a bewildered look and, without skipping a beat, looks back around at me, but now with questions written all over his face. I just give him that look of don't ask, I can't tell, and Bryce shuts the door. "*Before you say anything, I need to get back to work, so if you don't mind.*" Waving my hand towards the door in a swift manner, hoping he gets the point.

I grab my coat and grab Cole by the arm to rush him out of my office. *If I wasn't so direct with him, I would never get him to leave.* As we head down the hall to the elevator Cole tries to stall and talk with Blake at her desk *"not now Cole we have places to be and people to see lets go."* Shoving him into the elevator I tell Cole *"I'll call him later and that I'll take a rain check for lunch."* As I watch Cole's face disappear behind the elevator door closing, I remember I need my phone and it is on my desk.

Running back to my desk to grab my phone, I see Bryce come out of my office. As he shuts the door, he looks at me and says "I *just wanted to show my appreciation and I left a little something on your desk."* He leaves and I open the door to see what he could have put in there and there was a white envelope sitting right in the middle of the desk with my name on it. I open it and it is a check along with a card that states, "In *case you don't know, you're appreciated."* Placing the card in the drawer and closing it, almost forgetting to lock it, I slide the key in and turn it closed. Leaving the room, I scurry as fast as I can to my car. Getting in, I set the GPS address going to Mrs.White's home. Good lord, it is all the way across town and nowhere that I have been. A million lights and stop signs later I pull up to the curb seeing this home and having the notion that this might have been our victims safe haven, her comfort, her peace just knowing that her life ended so violently is enough to give me chills when I think about having to go in alone. Waiting on the front steps with not one care in the world is a lady dressed in a business suit and holding a large manilla envelope waiting for what I assume is me. I walk up and she reaches out a hand to shake and introduces herself and without further conversation she has me sign a release and hands me the envelope and leaves.

Taking the keys slowly out of my pocket and unlocking the door feels like eternity passing by in my mind. *It is baffling how everyone is going about their day, as if there wasn't a person murdered in this home yesterday. Just passing by and no one to miss her. That is one of my biggest fears in life dying and no one caring or knowing till it's too late.* With that thought leaving my mind, I step over the threshold of the door frame and into a dark and disheveled living area. A sudden jump scare knocks me off my game when a screeching of a cat goes haywire around my feet and, as you would guess, I scream. Knocking back into a large china cabinet that seems out of place in the center of the entryway.

Telling myself *to get a hold of my nerves* because this is the first case I'm doing alone since my partner is out on maternity leave. Thinking *about how jobs go much smoother when you actually work with someone you get along with. So doing this case alone seems like double duty, with no one actively watching my six.*

Reaching for the nearest light, I switch it on and begin to examine my surroundings of the scene. Going through my mental checklist, checking the door frames and windows to make sure if they were locked or for any broken glass. Scanning for anything that would be out-of-place other than where the body was or where the struggle took place. Seeing the blood stained rug and a bullet hole in the floor where the EMS found the victim sent the hairs on my neck standing straight up. Thanking *this world is so hard to live in these days. You really don't know a person or what they are capable of doing to someone.*

I take my phone out to notate what I see, when rounding the corner of the dining room I find the rug corner turned over. *Trying to understand why this was missed and not in the report, did they just miss this? Maybe with the amount of people in such a small proximity helped it goes unseen.*

Noticing an unusual seam pattern cut into the wood floor, I know I need to pull up the rug to check. *Why would the pattern change under the dining room table?* Taking out my phone, to record the whole dining room before I disturb any furniture in my investigation. I slowly push all the furniture out of the way. As I begin to pull the area rug aside, realizing that the floor has a doorway hatch cut into it.

Curiosity always gets the cat or so I'm told. I grab the sunken latch to open the heavy door, not knowing what I am getting myself into. But at this point, I have had no indication of anyone coming back in here. *I will just wait to see what I find.* A damp draft rushes out of the gaping hole that I am standing over when the door slams to the floor, causing a loud echo.

Using my flashlight to light up the doorway realizing there is a passage of wooden stairs leading into something like a tunnel, basement or unfinished cellar. I cautiously climb down into the narrow passage that seems like it has been here for the longest time, untouched. Even the air seems to begin to get thicker which makes it harder to breathe as I inch my way into the darkness. There is an awful stench in the air that aids in me getting lightheaded from the thickness of the air the farther along I go. Panicking, realizing that *I'm not going to make it to the end of the tunnel whether I go back or lord knows try to get to the other end.* In the distance, a voice so faint it's hard to hear it startles me, causing me to stumble over my own feet. My body begins to suddenly feel slow and heavy, making me fall to the ground. Panic sets in at an all time high and my mind begins to focus on my heartbeat that begins to slow down. That's when everything fades to black.

It's so dark and cold that I'm shivering uncontrollably. I don't know where I am, but it's not where I was when I couldn't breathe and everything suddenly went dark. Sitting up from the floor that I found myself laying on, I take in my surroundings. I notice while I'm on the floor of a bathroom that blood is coming from my head. Touching my head makes the pain insurmountable to anything I've felt before radiate throughout. I mean, I have had concussions before, but man, it's pounding. While I gather my thoughts I look around, this is not a surrounding I am familiar with. This bathroom is not where I was as I began to slowly stutter the sentence when it finally came out, "*Where am I?*"

The room is small and has a pedestal sink with a toilet next to the bathtub that has a rusty ring around the base where the silicone is missing. The floor is cold and textured, causing the grout to be a dark stained color that looks dirty. Wiping my hands on my clothes, I attempt to stand up climbing to my feet by grabbing the sink one hand at a time. Pulling myself up, I catch a glimpse of myself in the mirror to see how bad the wound is to my head. It is pounding and I can feel what seems to be a knot on it.

What the Hell is going on here? As I'm staring into the mirror, I stumble back against the wall into a towel rack, hitting the back of my head yet once again. I don't recognize the person staring back at me. I move, she moves; I talk, she talks! My brain can't process what is going on and what to do? Takes me a long good look into the mirror before I snap out of the shock.

I know I'll call Bryce for help. We'll see what he has to say. Maybe someone is behind this, maybe I've lost my mind! Nevermind he would probably think I'm nuts when he hears I was in a tunnel under the dining room and woke up in a bathroom with a bloody head not recognizing myself in the mirror. Who knows, he might not even recognize me at this point.

Again, *what is going on?*

Octavia C. Penn

Searching for clues as to where I am, I head to the living room of the apartment that I am in and see a photo out of the corner of my eye. Coming to a quick halt, I study the photo. *Wait, I know who that is.* More than a dozen images from the police profiles begin to race back and forth in my head as I close my eyes. My mind stops on one image. A Photo of her was on the news station last week. She has the same MO as Jennifer White. *What was her name.....*

Searching and searching for an answer, it appears on an envelope of a bill on the entryway table; It was addressed to a Sara. Sara was a single female that was home alone when she answered the door of her apartment, thinking it was her food delivery.

So how am I in her apartment and how is it I look like her?

Now in a panic phase, *what do I do?*

Call Cole?

Go home?

*No, there is a reason I'm here. I just need to stay and figure this out!*I turn the television on and flick it to the news station to see if there's an update to yesterday's events. So stressed out with my head pounding from earlier events of me in the passageway that for some reason I can't piece it together. "*I went down in that passageway; It was dark; the air was thick and suffocating, lanterns were there to light the walkway, as if it was used frequently. Then everything went downhill quickly from there on in. So strange how ...*" A knock at the door startles me.

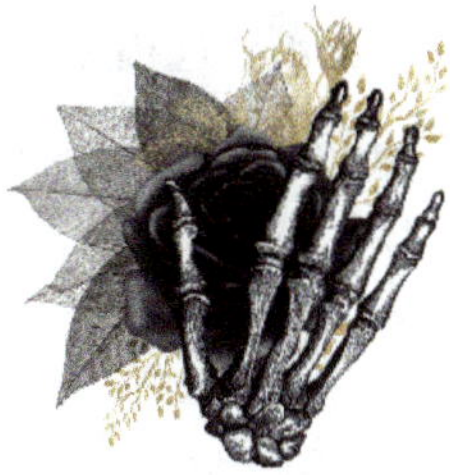

BRYCE

The door opens with a quick glance and my eyes stop, looking into the face of pure beauty. Not that she would ever be one to confirm my thoughts. I have never known her to react to anything a man thinks of her at this point in my lead of administration. She walks in looking annoyed, closing the door behind her. Paying no mind to her demeanor I can't seem to focus my thoughts when she enters a room. Someone as stunning as Jane ought to know just what she does to any person that she gets close to. This is the perfect meaning to simple and elegant beauty.

"Come in, Jane, have a seat."

I hand a file to her that isn't very full. This case was assigned to us this morning. I smile a slight grin to try and lighten the mood when I say, *"You are now the lead on it."*

"You are the person I'd like to see on this case, if you don't mind. Your attention to detail is needed at this moment. I am also aware your partner is on maternity leave, so if you need any assistance. All you need to do is just call."

The look in her eyes as I tell her I am in service to her in any way, shape, or form gives me chills. Okay, maybe not meant in that manner.

Jane leaves my office and closes the door behind her, leaving me to my vices. How she gripped the handle in a pissed but calm manner lets me know she is fed up with my shit. The phone rings as soon as she leaves, and it is the bank telling me that there will be someone with the key to Mrs. White's home wanting to meet with us.

Leaving the office to give the message to Jane when I notice out of the corner of my eyes that her friend is steam rolling down the hall to her office, not giving two cares in the world. I linger behind just a minute to watch and to give her time to throw him out or conduct her business; I stall by turning to talk to Blake at her reception desk.

Blake is a young woman that pretty much walked in and demanded that I gave her the job and I liked that. She would take no shit from any of the men. So I just hired her on the spot. It has worked every day since.

"Blake, how is your day?"

Blake looks up from her energy drink and gives me a blank stare into my soul.

"It is going slow, but good. Why are you asking?"

As she is speaking to me, I turn my head toward Jane's office to see if the door is open and the little meeting is done. Blake clears her throat and gives me a stern look.

"If you need anything, I'll be right here." She slides her headphones over her ears and carries on. *It was almost like she didn't care that I was her boss and needed anything. I don't, besides a cover.*

Not being able to wait any longer to give her this message and let her know I need her to get going as soon as possible. I turn to head down the hall, knocking on the door and relaying the message.

It is approaching five o'clock as I am leaving the office for the day as I wonder if Jane might need my help at the house so I decide I'm going to ride over and see what progress she has made. Having not heard from her all day makes me wonder what she has found or if she has run into any problems. I know she is the kind of person who likes to do things her way, but if she needs my help, I told her to ask. Maybe I just need to show up anyways just to prove to her I meant what I said. As I pull up at the house, the front door is wide open and no signs of Jane outside. Climbing the stairs I enter the home and clear the front foyer next to the living area where the crime took place, then I turn the corner of the dining room I see a rug pulled back and an entrance to what appears to be a hole to a cellar or basement. Worried about what I might find, I panic a little and grab my pistol from the holster, along with my flashlight.

Okay, Bryce, it might not be as bad as I may picture this scenario, so let's go. Leaning into the darkness with my wits about me and armed ready for whatever I see, there is a long tunnel and some wooden stairs. The space surrounding the tunnel is dark and eerie and with Jane missing to begin which has my stomach in knots. Until I have a definitive answer, I shouldn't let my mind wander to places unknown yet. There seem to be lanterns along the wall, as if someone uses this to hide from someone or to move something without being seen. This tunnel is dark and damp with no end in sight and with a dusty, dirty floor. I can see footprints going in both directions, so it must lead somewhere.

The further I go, I realize I might need to call for backup, so instead of endangering myself or Jane, I'm going to head back up and see if Jane is anywhere else in the house before I go any further.

As I slowly turn, I catch a glimpse of an object out of the corner of my eye. I study the object and notice it's some type of large tank chained to the wall. Tetrachloroethane is what the tanks read. looking around, there are about a dozen of them scattered around me. So I snap a picture using my phone and head back up to the dining room. Something about this whole case is hitting differently from any other case I have covered. My gut is telling me that something is wrong and it is normally right about these situations. Something isn't right and I'm going to sort this out, but First Jane.

Climbing out of the floor of the dining room, I hear someone holler out for Jane. "*Jane*!" Pausing for a second, I roll my eyes. "Here we go" shrugging and shaking my head. I try to understand why he is showing up at the crime scene? He has no sense of space or personal boundaries.

Rounding the doorway was Cole, Jane's Friend. *How did he even know where to find her?* With an empty expression on his face, he meets me in the living room holding lunch in his hand. I snarled at Cole, proceeding to tell him *"That he can't be here. This is a crime scene that him being here is impeding the investigation."*

Why are you here? How did you even know where to find her? Jane isn't supposed to tell anyone about the case.

Coles' response to my questions are short and to the point. *"Well, she didn't but with all the commotion about there might be a serial killer loose, I figured she was here. The last known place the killer was considering that you pulled her vacation for an emergency!"*

To be honest, I can't stand him, so I'm not really paying too much attention. I tell him that *"I will take the food and give it to Jane, letting her know you brought it for her."* Grabbing Cole by the arm, I pushed him out the door. I turn to sit the food on the entryway table and holler for Jane.

"Jane!" clearing every room, panicking because I can't seem to locate her anywhere in the home, knowing that her car is parked out front and she didn't leave. I call her phone over and over, trying to give myself a logical explanation on where she will be I get her voicemail.

"Hi this is detective Slone leave your name and number and I'll get back with you."

"Jane, this is Bryce. I'm here at the house. Your car is out front but I can't seem to locate you. I did find the tunnel that you uncovered in the dining room. call me as soon as you get this. I will be here till you do."

As the night creeps in I decide to call it a night and head back to the office in hopes maybe there was car trouble and she called a cab back . As I turn to shut the door I hear a thud and some rattling in the distance. Startled thinking it was Jane I paused and hollered *"Jane!"* pausing to catch my breath and looking back in the direction of the noise I see a slight light flicker that comes out from the tunnel under the dining room floor.

Waiting for a few seconds I am hopeful, wishing and staring at that hatch in the floor waiting for Jane to magically appear but with no movement I turn to leave grabbing the door handle to close up the house. Thinking to myself that it was just my imagination.That is when I hear Jane's voice come from behind me. *"Leaving me already?"*

Turning as fast as I could to see Jane standing in the dining room looking like a train wreck. With a knot on her head and blood on her clothes and face I dare ask what happened when she gives me a slight grin. One of relief, one of safety. I could suddenly breath with ease but also at the same time pissed that she scared me like she did. *Where has she been and what was she doing?* At this point I am tired and emotionally tapped out so I'm just going to tell her to *"go home and I'll see her in the morning bright and early with a report about today ready for me on my desk."* I can't put too much emotion into it or I might just explode from all the emotions at once. Never in a million years did I ever think I could be this invested in another person.

She pauses for a second and confused with the look on her face of defeat she basically just shrugs and walks past me. As if I let her down. I follow her out the door and to the street's edge watching her get in and sit in her car. She sits there for a moment when I decide to get her out of her head space and knock on the window to shout *"go home Jane!"*

Octavia C. Penn

Making sure she is okay in her car I wait and watch as she leaves. The drive around town to Jane's house has me in a protective mode for her. Wanting to do just that I tell myself *"If she wants me to stay with her tonight I will gladly accept the invitation."* because lord knows she looked a bit shaken and beat up. *Maybe she will tell me what happened once she has time to get home in her safe space.*

Cole and Richard

Pulling up to Jane's work in hopes of getting her to come eat lunch with me has my stomach at an unease. Knowing that I am about to deceitfully tell her I want to take her to lunch to get her out of the rut she calls life has me second guess my loyalty to Richard.

"Jane," I yell as I open her office door, throwing myself down in one of her office chairs. Giving her a lecture about eating, she just rolls her eyes and lets me ramble like a nagging parent. *"Don't make me pack your lunch like a child that needs their mother."* As I say with a shit-eating grin on

my face, knowing she will bite back with more than an average response. That is what I love about her: we can nitpick with one another and not take it personally.

The knock on the door interrupts us as Bryce clears the doorway with an agenda for Jane and it knocks my plans out of the water so fast Jane basically grabs me up from her office chair and rushes me to the elevator without hesitation. As the elevator door closes with me inside, I call Richard to tell him that I couldn't get Jane to lunch but I could tell him where she would be for the next few hours. Richard jumps at the chance to tell me to "follow her and make sure I stay away from the house and if she heads back to call and tell him."

"She will be at Jessica's house to do an initial walk through for her investigation." The line went silent as I waited for a response. The silence on the other end of the phone was

suspicious and made me uneasy. *"Whatever the fact is, she won't be home and that will work out just fine."* As Richard ends the conversation on the phone, he tells me to *"Watch her and meet me tonight."* He makes it clear he has some kind of big news to tell me.

Pulling up to the corner of 62nd and Kennedy St. I see Jane going into the house. To not let her see me, I pull around to the house on the back of the property and watch through the chain-link fence from the neighboring houses. Some time seems to pass as the sun goes down behind the tree line across from the park when I see the great and annoying Mr. Bryce himself make an appearance.

"What is he doing?"

Getting out of the car, I grab what was left of mine and Jane's lunch and make haste to the house. I see this as my alibi, my out if something goes south.

"Bryce," he turns around and gives me a blank stare and immediately asks me, *"What am I doing at this house?"* Feeds me the line of I'm *"Impeding an investigation and contaminating a crime scene just being there."* So I responded with, *"You interrupted our lunch earlier in the day and I wanted to give Jane a meal. Is that a crime?"* As usual in Bryce fashion, he takes the lunch and tells me along the lines of *"get lost and I'll let her know you brought the food."*

Man handling me, he shoves me out the door and I turn to give him a go to hell look, but he is already on to other things, not looking in my direction. So I head back to my car and I just wait like Richard ordered me to.

With about half an hour that goes by and I see the front door open wide with Bryce standing alone in the doorway. He hesitates for a minute and then spins around faster than I could register when I see him waving his arms in a punishing motion. My only guess would be if Jane did something he didn't approve of and he's scolding her for it. Watching this whole scenario play out, Jane leaves the doorway and makes her way down the steps to her car with this wild and empty look upon her face.

Guess this case is more than she can handle, figuring that's what the fight was about. Jane gets in the car and leaves with Bryce not far behind her as I get on the phone and text Richard.

"She is done Jane is on her way. Get out now!"

Jane

I hesitate as the rap at the door increases in volume, wondering if I should answer it at all considering that I'm not me, or am I in my right mind? Who knows, this could all be a dream, a bad dream that I will wake up from at any moment. Reaching for the chain lock on the door, unlocking it, I turn the handle slightly pulling it ajar, all the while I ask who it is. I get the response *"I have your food for delivery"* the man grunts with a low ominous tone.

As soon as I open the door, this man goes to hand me the bag. Just as I go to grab it, he raises his leg and kicks me in the gut. Which has now shoved me into the apartment and onto the floor. Food flying in all directions around me with the sounds of chaos ensuing, I try to catch my breath and climb to my feet. Noticing the man in the doorway stepping through the frame and shutting the door behind him and attaching the chain lock.

This man seems kinda tall with a medium build and wearing normal clothing. It is a little too dark to be able to see any of his other features. Thinking to myself, is this a distraught lover, an angry co-worker or a neighbor? What could I have done to make someone this angry? Sliding backward across the floor, trying to move away from him as he approaches me, I encounter a table.

The man crouches down over me as I am buckled over on the floor, gasping for air and a sense of direction when the man leans over and grabs me by the back of my hair and drags me down the hallway. Kicking and screaming as he struggles to get me where he wants me. He stops and turns around and decks me in the face, not once, but twice. For the moment, I stop screaming and I begin to cry. He places his hand around my throat to choke me a little and gets as close as possible to my face in a controlling manor

"There you go, shut your pretty little mouth like a good girl," he growls in a low, frighting tone.

That shit hurts more than I could take at this moment. Wondering when someone might hear me and help? Tears streaming down my face and blood seeping out of my mouth where his fist made my lip cut on my teeth.

Continuing down the hallway with me in tow by the hair, just this time with both hands. He stops at the doorway, then drops the top half of me to the floor; he turns to open the door to the bedroom. Giving me the opportunity to take that as my way to get up and run, but he is too fast. He yanks me back down by my hair. My body just crumbles like a stack of cans getting knocked over. Turning around and pulls out what I think are some zip ties, he aggressively turns me over, kneeling down on top of me where I'm face down on the floor. Panicking, thinking about what he is about to do, I try to run, but he gets on top of me one arm at a time. As I am struggling with him, I hear a very loud popping noise. The heat from searing pain and then a numbing feeling as he is placing both hands in the zip ties. This man tightens them so tight I begin to lose feeling in them.

There it goes. I can feel it burning and the throbbing sensation of pain shooting through my shoulder and arm.

From what I believe is my arm being popped out of the socket from sheer force and bad luck.

"I can't believe this is happening to me" This is all I could think of at this point, so I scream even louder, hoping someone has heard this god-awful scenario playing out in this apartment. Searching through the draws of the room, he pulls out a sock. He now places it as a gag in my mouth and tapes it shut by running the tape across my mouth and around my head. Thinking, *"How am I going to survive this?"*

He then takes a knife out and begins to cut my clothing from my body, starting with my shirt. This whole time with his knee in my back as he begins to cut the jeans from my waist. Not being careful, he nicks me and I start to bleed. Hold Still, he mumbles as he is struggling to complete this task. Not wanting to give him the satisfaction of getting what he wants, I continue to struggle. He reaches down and places his hand over my nose to try and suffocate me as he says, *"If you won't just be quiet and still I will make you"* he lets go just in time that I don't black out. Closing my eyes, I try focusing on myself and my muffled cries for help. Trying to not give him another reason to strike me again, I now remember my fate as I am not me in this reality. *I am Sara; I know how this is going to end for me. Who is this and why? Why am I in this apartment and this lady's body for this moment? Why me? What could I possibly do to change her fate?*

Feeling this man run his hands all over me as he pulls what's left of the clothing from my body, he stops. The room goes quiet and only the stifled breathing from the struggle could be heard. With fear everything goes silent and I hear this man take a step backward, undoing his belt, listening to the rattling and clanking of the metal against each other.

Not being able to see him or what he plans to do is mind-numbing and frightening. I hear a squeak of the bed when I assume it is him sitting down on it. I am listening to hear what is going on, but it is nothing but him moaning. What sounds like him staring at my body from a distance, taking advantage of the view to please himself.

Remembering my training about sexual and physical abuse, most victims that can't get out of it shut down or turn off their emotions to escape the situation. Never having to be a person who has had to do that before, I was hoping it would just take over, that I wouldn't have to deal with this mans wrath and torture. As the struggle becomes apparent that he finished with himself, I hear the bed squeak. He gets up and his heavy feet stomp across the floor towards me, hoping he is done. He then kneels on top of me and gets so close I can smell him. The scent of musk and leather as he then takes his hand and puts it against my face. Running the back of his hand down the side of my cheek like he is petting me. He then takes his penis in his hand and forces it in between my legs, forcing them apart, and aggressively slamming his body against mine. He takes his arm and slides it under me around my neck and pulls me harder into him. Tears rolling down my face and breathing harder, trying to not stay in this moment, he groans into my ear to *"Just be a good girl and take it."*

Feeling the pain from the beating and the burning from the knife that cut me, I start to hyperventilate from the weight of the man on top of me as he is slamming his body violently against me so hard I think to myself *he is crushing me.*

My breathing was rapid, but it is now so slow I don't know if I'm breathing or almost suffocating. Like there is not enough air in the room. My skin goes cold and I start shaking uncontrollably. My mind began to slip into yesterday morning when I was in my sunroom sitting on the chair taking in the quiet of the morning, where I was happy and safe, not here.

His hands now wrapping around my neck, he chokes me, baring down harder with every second till I no longer can breathe any sort of way. The light of the room fades as I choke, causing the surrounding scene to pulse black with my heart beat as I struggle to breathe. Tears running down my face, with my thoughts racing, everything goes dark, and I am gone.

I hear a noise in the distance that echoes from a door being shut. It's dark and I start choking on the dusty air. I become aware of my surroundings. So confused as to what is going on, I shuffle toward the wall so I am sure to see any surprises if they come at me.

Where is he?

Did he carry me down to the tunnel?

Did I hallucinate this whole thing?

I could imagine this sounding insane to anyone that I try to explain this to. Gathering myself to get to my feet, I hold on to the wall noticing that I am in a small space like room but it's not any place I've seen. The surroundings are similar to the passageway that I found under Jessica's dining room floor. It has a dirt floor that is dark and damp with lanterns along the wall, but this room has a bed in it. *Maybe this is at the other end or another area altogether.*

Hearing a faint cry in the distance, I slowly make my way closer to where the noise is coming from. The closer that I get, the better I can hear.

It's Bryce. Why is he here?

Hollering back, I realize my voice is crackling and rough sounding, so I run to make it back to the beginning of this tunnel and get the hell out of here. *I'm getting closer*, as I can see the stairs that lead to the dining room that is lit by the light of the house. I slow down just for a second.

Turning around to make sure no one was behind me, I turn my phone light on and scanned the tunnel. Stopping just long enough to take in the surroundings of the nightmare once more.

Why? Is all I can think of when in my head my brain is screaming to get out of here as fast as humanly possible.

Climbing the stairs to the hatch, I then see Bryce standing in the doorway of the house and I holler his name *"Bryce!"*

Thanking god that it is him and not that monster. Bryce turning in disbelief his face looks pale but with a sigh of relief, then of anger. *"Where were you? I looked all over for you calling your name, phone and nothing. I was worried, don't scare me like that!"*

Waiting for my response, he says *"Never mind,"* He then gives me a look over and then tells me *"To go home. I will see you in the morning. You look like you have been through hell and back."*

With the only logical response, I say, *"You don't have a clue."* Wanting to go home and process all that I just went through, I shake my head and respond, *"See you in the morning."* With my feet planted on the top step, I turn to look at Bryce, thinking, I don't want to be alone after what I just went through. I'm scared to be. Not saying another word, I just turn to quickly get to my car.

Jane

Getting in my car, as I am visibly shaking. While I sit here for a few moments to catch my breath and take in the ordeal that had just taken place in that death ridden house. *Or did it?* At this moment, I'm not sure what I believe really happened to me. Trying to put what happened out of my mind so I could clearly and safely drive home.

But I catch myself frozen with my hands gripped together so tightly my knuckles start to turn white. As the images of being tied down like a feral hog and brutally raped and murdered flash through my mind at an alarming rate. *Well, Sara was from what I am assuming.* Shaking my head when a sudden beating on the window catches my attention. It was Bryce. *"Go home,"* he shouts through the glass window.

I place the car in drive, slide my foot off of the brake and onto the gas pedal, accelerating slowly. Making my way around the block and back onto the main road. I head toward my house where I can unravel the dreadful events of the day. Passing all the familiar shops and cafes as I get closer. Knowing that I put some distance between myself and that place helped me relax just enough to loosen my grip on the steering wheel. As I pull up to my brownstone, all the lights are off except for the porch light, that is dimly lighting the steps. *I need to get a better fixture for the stoop, so it is not casting so many shadows* muttering to myself. It is funny how one event can change the world and your views all at once. Even when they have been there in front of you the whole time.

Sitting there in my car as it quietly idles, I notice Bryce pulling in behind me. Guessing I wasn't as clear-headed on my drive home as I would have normally been. Because for the thirty minutes it took me to get home, I did not notice him following me. Bryce stops with about half a car distance between us and turns the headlights off. Making it easier to see that it was him. Bryce gets out and walks up to my side of the vehicle. Watching him the whole time thinking, *I can't argue about work right now. What could be his reason for following me home?* Reaching down to turn the car off, I grab my bag to get out when Bryce grabs my door handle to open the door and startles me. That notion of calmness was gone in a single breath of air when I gasped out of sheer fright. Bryce has already made it to my car door and gallantly opens it before I had the chance.

"*Bryce,*" I exclaimed, "*you can't just open someone's door in the middle of the night!*"

All he was doing was gallantly opening my door, and I took it out on him.

"*Bryce,* my voice crackles with every word I attempt to force out of my mouth, *I'm alright you didn't have to follow me home.*" With a worried expression on his face, he pulls me up from the car. Looking me over as he pulls me in and, without a single warning, he hugs me and kisses me on the forehead. "*The way we left Jessica's house had me so uneased, I needed to know what happened,*" Bryce calmly responded. He doesn't move or shift, but that is okay at this moment. His smell and embrace makes my walls come down with a flood of tears. I don't think he was thinking about what he was doing when he kissed me because it almost felt like a natural instinct had taken over. Grabbing the back of his shirt, pulling him in closer with my arms tightly wrapped around him, I let out an awful scream as all the pain mentally and physically set in. Bryce just squeezes harder, embracing me, not knowing what to do or say. Letting me have this moment to release everything I have bottled up for the past few hours. He looks at me, wipes a few of the tears off my cheek.

Looking into Bryce's eyes, I see a different side of him come to life. Bryce's eyes glass over and his facial features tense in a serious manner. "*Jane,*" he quietly says, "*whatever happened today is over and you are home safe. I don't know what happened to you in that house, but you need to tell me. You have it written all over your face that you just were through something hellish. I had to see for myself you made it safely home.*"

The sky lights up with a flash of lightning and thunder rumbles across the sky, giving me chills all across my body. Taking in a sigh of deep breath, I step back and look at him. The distance causes an awkward silence, and the air stiffens. Looking him in his blue eyes, I whisper *"Goodnight"* trying to control my voice's emotions. That is all that I could fathom to get out of my mouth, as it felt like I couldn't speak. Thinking at this moment *that my mind is so scrambled that I don't even know what I want.* The thoughts of Bryce coming to my aid and being my knight and shining armor following me home to make sure I was safe made me weak in my knees. I could just melt into his arms if I knew it wouldn't be an awkward rejection as fast as I moved to do so. *I mean, I don't know if it was just worry or if he was just doing his job and got caught up in my emotions when he kissed me? Who knows? All of this could just be wishful thinking I suppose.* The thought of me wanting him to come in and stay with me tonight quickly proceeded with the first thoughts in my head. Thinking to myself, *this is just him being a good man and nothing to do with him having feelings for me. It could just be me projecting this onto him and I'm overthinking this, like I said, wishful thinking I suppose.*

Leaving his side, I begin the walk up the stairs to my front door. With a quick glance behind into the dark street to see if he stayed until I got in the door. Another flash of lightning shoots across the night sky and this time when the thunder hits it shakes me to my core. The sky empties as the rain begins to fall. Landing on my face as I close my eyes, looking up into the night sky. It is as if it is washing away all the madness that was crawling on my skin. Just for a moment, the world didn't exist, nothing existed and nothing else mattered. Feeling like I survived a nightmare when out of the blue I hear *"Jane"* startled. I turn to see him standing at the base of the stairs looking at me. Soaking wet all the same as me and says, *"I can't leave without knowing you are fine. Not just okay, but fine."* Bryce was staring at me, almost like he could read my thoughts and see into my soul *"ask me to stay."* The pause was so intense causing the moment to be deafening he began to quietly stutter "*unless…*" When the corner of my mouth raises to show a notion that, that is what I wanted all along. Bryce steps forward and meets me on the top step, embracing me in a kiss. It was a truly magical moment filled with such raw emotion and intensity. As the rain drizzled down, we found ourselves standing under the stoop light. It provided a warm glow amidst our deep, dark surroundings.

Bryce, with his dark hair soaked from the rain with his deep blue eyes that seem to only glisten brighter in the flickering light, had me so mesmerized that I could feel both of our hearts beating faster as we embraced each other.

The sound of the rain falling around us created a small moment in time where it was only us. The air was charged with anticipation, as if nature itself was hinting at the bonded chemistry between us. As if we were meant to be, like two star-crossed lovers in the night.

Turning to catch my breath, I reach for the keys to unlock the door. When I turn back around, the image of him is so breathtaking that I can't resist the pull of his desire any longer. Bryce takes a step closer to me, closing the already narrow distance between us. Taking another deep breath, I swallow so hard I think even the Gods could hear. He Reaches out and gently brushes a strand of hair out of my face. Leaving his fingers lingering on my cheek, feeling the warmth radiating from his skin.

Our eyes locked in the moment, and if it wasn't any clearer, it is now. It made any unspoken doubts and feelings that were now very apparent. Bryce leaned in, placing his head against mine. I could see the desire and feel his vulnerability like a current of electricity running through me.

That, in this moment, he put us in a peculiar predicament. *I'm not going to complain though, as I am enjoying the attention.*

Bryce cupped my face in his hands, sending the sensations of a shiver down my body. A soft gasp escaped from my lips as he tilted his head closer and gently pressed his lips once more to mine. With a whirlwind of emotions from the both of us, we couldn't stop. The kiss was a dance of passion with so much intensity that it did nothing but pour fuel to the fire.

Finally pulling away from me like it was the hardest thing he had to do. Bryce just smiled at me, touching his fingers to his lips. With rain-soaked clothes and my heart full of joy, he holds both of my hands and leans forward to kiss them ever so slightly.

"I don't have to stay if you would rather be alone tonight or change your mind." We both smile. I am so glad that he feels the same way I do.

With the world faded away around us and both of us lost in the moment. I lean in and whisper into his ear "*come on, let's get out of the rain before we both end up sick."* Bryce smiles ear to ear as if he has waited forever and a day to hear those words come out of my mouth.

Octavia C. Penn

Jane turns to go inside and Bryce grips ahold of her hand and gives her the most calm but forced response. *"I should probably go."* With a surprised look on my face, *"I thought you wanted to stay. I thought you wanted to spend the night, to keep me safe? Am I wrong?"*

Leaning in, Bryce places one hand on my cheek and his rain drenched lips against mine. *The taste of him as the rain washes over the both of us is intoxicating. "I will stay for a while, but you need your rest and you can't do that if I stay."* He nods his head toward the house to give me the notion that we would be up all night. *"I will come back in the morning to check on you."* Squeezing my hand one last time, I watch as Bryce turns to leave.

"Bryce,"

He turns around and I wave goodnight, trying to convince myself to not look through the window, but I can't help myself. *He is still there, maybe I should insist he come inside, this is my chance.* With my thoughts racing my better judgment takes a hold and decides for me to leave well enough alone. Not wanting to ruin a perfect ending to a horrible day I see Bryce drive away. Now that I am alone, leaving me with my thoughts to unravel inside my mind and body.

Looking around the foyer I see a mess where I currently have everything dropped onto the floor, not caring if it would trip someone later or hell, maybe even me. *It may even deter an intruder if that ever comes to fruition.*

Deep sigh as I step over everything and make my way to the kitchen to grab a bag of pretzels with chocolate humus and a glass of wine. I need something to snack on and to calm my nerves all at once, then head up to the bathroom for a relaxing soak in my tub. Entering the bathroom, turning on the water making sure it is the perfect mix of hot and steamy and waiting for it to fill, I check to see if I could handle it as I take my clothes off and my hair down.

"*Perfect,*" I said, turning on the television for some noise and lighting some candles then I went into the tub. Nodding off, scared to fall asleep in the tube, I daydream of a better tomorrow. Thinking *nothing could be worse than this day,* I scrub my body by lathering my favorite vanilla and apricot soap on my loofah, wincing as it glides over the sore spots on my body.

What about this torture I endured as Sara made it so realistic, like it happened to me to my actual body? At the time, I didn't believe it left any marks or bruises. Until time and adrenaline passed, and I just didn't notice the dried blood on the temple of my face until I caught a glimpse of myself in the mirror as I swept my hair back in a hair tie. I began to wash my face. Washing everything from head to toe, I hear the news go off with breaking news. *Nope, I don't care at this point to get out of the tub.* Debating with myself.

Time passes and the water begins to temper when my phone vibrates and lights up the dimly lit bathroom. Taking a deep sigh, I take this as my sign to get out and call it a night. Pulling the plug on the tub, I stand dripping wet as I wrap my towel around me and another for my hair, stepping out of the tub as the water drains. Staring at myself in the mirror as I am drying off, I can see my face bruising, looking away as fast as I see the marks. I gather my clothes and head to the bedroom to climb into my bed. Forgetting that my phone had a message, I lean over to place it on the charger when I see it is a message from Bryce it reads.

I would have stayed, but you deserve better, someone who would put your needs first. Get you some rest and I will see you in the morning.

"*Great.*" *Now all that relaxing is out the window and my mind is racing. I definitely should have insisted that he come in with me.* That lifts my heart up so much it almost masks the physical pain that is seeping in all at once.

The next morning I lay in the bed wide awake as if I never went to sleep, with thoughts racing back and forth like a dog on a leash. It's no wonder I didn't get any sleep at all. I roll over in my bed and grab my phone laying there quietly. With the daunting task of having to adult today, I typed an email to Bryce telling him that I'm taking the day off here to get my draft ready and I'll be in at seven in the morning. That's when we can go over all of last night's events. Eyes puffy and exhausted, I don't quite remember falling asleep. With a knock on the door filling the halls, sounding an alarm with the heavy-handed knock, I leap to my feet and grab my robe and pistol before heading down the stairs. Cautiously peering out of the peephole making sure it's not someone after me, I see it's a police officer and a marked car at the end of the drive. Thinking this has something to do with last night, I take a deep breath and decide I'm going to open it.

Bryce

The sun peering into the room shining into my eyes as the alarm rings into the abyss of my tired mind. I lay there with the thoughts of last night. *They were emotionally exhausting, and I wanted more to come of the situation, but I needed to let Jane know we could take it slow and that we could just call it a night. Even if I desperately wanted to stay, even if it was just to keep an eye on her. Having Jane's body close to mine meant she was safe and, after longing for her for the past six years, she was finally free to make her own choices.*

Turning over as the cool bed sheets graze my skin and raise the hair on my arms when the cool morning air touches them, my alarm sounds again. Never getting an answer from her about why she was in the tunnels yesterday makes me anxious about what I find out in our meeting today. Laying there for a moment longer, being as comfortable as I was daydreaming and almost drifting back to sleep, when my alarm goes off again, startling me making me realize I am more tired than I thought I could be. *Maybe it's me being emotionally drained over being physically drained. Who knows?*

"*Guess it's time to get up,*" saying out loud to give myself the motivation to move.

Thinking to myself, *I have plenty to take care of today. First off, I need to get to the office and get the full report from Jane on the events that unraveled last night and where she plans to go from here.* Walking to the shower, I catch a gimp of the clothes hanging over the top of the hamper that I was wearing last night when Jane hugged me. I noticed a small stain of red on the breast of the shirt. Guessing that I was so distracted and exhausted when I got home last night that I didn't see the stain in the dark of the night. Grabbing it to let it soak while I got a shower and noticed that it was not lipstick that it is actual blood. I knew something was worse off than she was letting on. This is a cause for a whole other level of concern. *I know I was mad, but it was mostly out of fear of not being able to find her. Hopeful that when I see her this morning that she can open up more about what she witnessed last night in that house. Hopeful that she can now trust me enough to know that she can be honest with me and tell me whatever she needs to.* Placing the shirt in my sink with hot water and a good amount of peroxide, intending to just let it soak while I shower and let the peroxide lift the stain before I wash it. *A little secret from having a sister.*

Getting into the shower that has been running hot for the past five minutes has my bathroom completely fogged over. With the stillness of the room and the sound of the water beating against the tile floor, I go over my day in my head. Almost sending myself into another world in my head, the reality of my phone ringing catches my attention and brings me back to the fog-dense room. With the cleaning process done and out of the way, I towel off and grab my jeans and button-up shirt and head for the bedroom. "*I don't feel like a suit today, just business casual it is.*" Talking to myself as I get dressed in the mirror.

Getting ready to leave the house for the day, I grab a protein bar, my lunch out of the fridge and keys off the table.With a little pep in my step, excited for what the day will bring, I head out the door. Wishing I knew exactly what happened last night in that house so I could comfort Jane because I have never seen her that way and nor do I ever want to again. She was so pale and shaken that I could hardly stand watching as she climbed out of the passageway door that was carved out in the floor. The scene is almost like something out of a horror movie. Pulling up at the office, I realize I drove all the way across town and paid little attention to how I got here almost on autopilot; it seems. My mind is not focused on work today, just Jane. I guess too much is going on and maybe getting this day started with a coffee and some breakfast for our meeting will kick me in the right gear.

Walking past the reception desk, I don't see Blake here yet, so it seems I will get on my phone and place an order myself for Jane and I. That is not a normal day for Blake. She is usually the first in and the last out on most occasions. Despite her age and her generation, she is very well organized and on top of her own life. So this is okay for today. She never asks for days off and always does what she can when I ask.*Now what is the name of the bagel place on the corner that we always order from?* Pacing back and forth in front of my desk, I hear '*Charlies*' loud and clear. It was Blake and just like that, she never skips a beat and sits down at her desk like she was here the whole time. It is strange how she just finished my sentence as if we were having the conversation together the whole time.

Anxiously waiting for Jane to walk through my office door, I keep busy by going through my case files and emails for the day. Every so often leaning over to the side of my desk to peer out the window next to the door wondering why Jane hasn't shown up yet. The day is almost halfway over when I hear a knock at the door and Blake announces when she enters the room that *"Jane will not be in the office today so that she can get caught up on her report before the day is done."* Stating, she has *"set a meeting for us tomorrow at 7am in her office."* Nodding at her response, I tell her *"to set the meeting and that it is fine with me."*

Worried that she is needing help with whatever she couldn't explain last night and with me finding the spot of blood on my shirt from her face gives me the bright notion to show up and bring coffee and breakfast just to be sure and check for myself she is fine.

Heading to the car, I notice the clouds in the distance getting heavier the farther away they appear to be. Reaching for the handle, I press unlock on my key fob and drop the keys, reaching down to grab them. I barely miss the side mirror with my head. *That's a close one*, thinking to myself. *Guess as long as I don't answer, I'm doing just fine.* A smirk on my face as I kinda chuckle at my joke, I get in and start the car.

Pulling out of the parking lot, the downpour begins with winds slightly, but quickly escalating. Struggling to drive down Main St. the rain goes from a drizzle to a downpour, making it hard to see with all the cars parked along the roads. Thinking out loud to myself, *"I hope no one steps out across the road trying to hurry across it in hopes of not getting as soaked by this storm."* I was approaching a four-way stop light. When a huge ball of ice hits my windshield and shatters it from one side to the other, impairing my vision even further than had it been just the rain. Which in turn causes me to hit my brakes, causing me to slide uncontrollably through the intersection and hit a light pole. The airbags then deploy within seconds and save my face from slamming into the steering wheel. Trying to shake off the effects of the impact of the crash, I look around to assess the damage. With rain hammering down onto the top of the car and droplets trickling down one by one, dropping to the pavement next to the shattered glass. Mixing with the faint smell of gasoline in the air and the car's smoke barreling out of the engine, I try to climb my way out of the car. The twisted metal of the hood and fender and the pole looming ominously over me I see a faint shapeless shadow like figure in the distance. It is almost unreal.

Reaching for the seat belt and clicking it, trying to force it to release. It won't come free, no matter how hard I try. With the mix of panic sinking in and coming down out of an adrenaline rush, I search for my phone to call for help.

Looking around the chaos of my surroundings, my phone is nowhere in sight or within reaching distance. When out of nowhere, I hear more screeching coming from far off. But this god-awful sound is rapidly approaching when I see the sight of two headlights. Then I realize that it's too late. Seeing the headlights dialing in on me coming from the opposite side of the four-way intersection, I brace myself for the impact. The headlights cast eerie shadows all around me when they hydroplane into my car. The sounds of metal crunching against metal as we collide together is deafening to my ears. The impact launched the car into the air, jolting me back and forth as oncoming traffic veers out of the way. Flipping end over end, causing me to collide with the side of a small building.

Listening to the sound of the car crumbling around me and the screaming of the metal scraping across the pavement, thinking, *I'm not going to make it out of this in one piece. What are the odds of me hitting a pole and getting hit by an out-of-control SUV causing me to slam into a brick building and me walking away okay without life-threatening injuries or even death?*

Coming to an abrupt stop upside down in a car that is crushed around you like someone stepping on a Coke can is not for the faint of heart. Everything is a blur and a mess of belongings from me and metal scraps torn from the car all around that I really don't know if I'm going to be okay. The taste of blood spewing from my mouth and gasping for more air than I can take in at the moment, a sharp pain in my chest arises when I try to breathe. Feeling like I was hit by a Mac truck, not an SUV, has me worried about the others in the secondary car. *Oh God, please let them be okay!*

Screaming desperately for help, my vision begins to fade in and out as the surrounding scene goes dark. I find it harder to stay awake and get myself out of this mess. Knowing that something is not right medically with me. As I am fighting to calm myself, all the while fighting for myself to stay awake is inevitable, but for a split second, I can hear someone ask if I'm okay. Everything aches as I strain to help them hold me up as they grab my seat belt to cut it with their pocket knife and free me from the seat. As gentle as they tried to be, my body slammed against the inside roof of the car and that's the last I can remember.

Jane

Quickly opening the door asking if everything is alright and how may I help him, the officer introduces himself and, with a grave look upon his face and pauses long enough to worry me.

"Mrs. Sloan?"

"*Yes*," I quickly responded. *"I have some news for you about a Mr. Gamble."*

Confused, I ask *"Okay, what is it?"*

"We arrived at the scene of an accident and with this chaotic weather that has been appearing all over town this morning has made Mr. Gamble end up in a really horrific accident. We had him life flighted to Memorial Hospital

downtown. We found his phone, and it had your name as his last contact in it. Would you come with me? I'll escort you to the hospital for some information."

Standing in this doorway with a police officer on the other side made a flood of memories race in and they reminded me of when I was told about my parents the night that they passed. My aunt that I hardly knew had to fly in from Texas to take care of me. I was all of 5 years old and blamed myself. Again, with the rain and water on the roadway, it is like someone is trying to send me a sign or playing a sick cosmic sized joke with my life.

Is this a way mother nature or God is trying to tell me that I don't get to have anyone in my life? That I'm meant to be alone, no friends, family, or confidants? That's just cruel and unusual punishment.

Asking if Bryce would make it, I shake the fear and grab my keys and phone, following quickly out the door after him. The ride to the hospital seemed to take the longest of time. It felt like every light we came to was red. Pulling up to the Emergency room door, I jump out and rush to the registration desk and ask to see Bryce Gamble. Explaining he was brought in by life flight she cut me off and explained that he is in surgery and it will be awhile. She then hands me a small sheet of paper with a six-digit code on it and says that I can follow the patient on a screen with that code and points to a section of chairs and asks me to have a seat and to wait till further news is relayed by the doctor.

My phone rings. Looking at the screen, I see a familiar name flash across. It's Cole. His Response as soon as I answer is "Are you okay?"

Relaying what the officer told me, I let him know I was at home, taking the day for myself after my long night of work. Wondering how he knew I was there, he said he came by the office and Bryce's assistant caught him in the hall and told him what had happened so now he was calling to see what he needed to do?

Nothing really just going to wait for an update on Bryce and then I'm sure there will be nothing I can do here for a while because when he comes out of surgery, I'm sure he will sleep off the effects of the anesthesia. Telling Cole I might just come into the office after this and put my mind on something other than what had happened to Bryce. Knowing when he wakes up, he is going to want an update on the case and I want to give him something.

Hours pass and a doctor nudges me awake in the waiting area and tells me to follow him. Leading me down a hall and rounding the corner past the nurses' desk to a room in the ICU, I follow him inside.

The shock on my face says more than I wanted it to when the doctor says, *"I can give you a minute if you need it and I'll come back."*

Leaping to a response, I tell him to tell me the truth about how bad the situation is. The doctor tells me he has a punctured lung and a brain bleed from the multiple collisions that took place with multiple cuts and bruises. Bryce also crashed on the table twice, so they placed him into a medically induced coma till his body heals. He also let me know they called his sister and she will be here tomorrow. Thanking him for keeping him alive, that he accomplished a miracle and we are all grateful.

The doctor leaves the room, closing the door behind him, and I turn to stare at Bryce laying in the bed with tubes coming out of every opening. He has so many cuts and bruises on his body and so much swelling that if I wouldn't have known better, I would have told you that the man in the bed wasn't Bryce at all. I slowly walk over to the bedside and lean in to whisper into his ear as if he can hear me. "*You have to rest and get better. I can't do this alone.*"

The images of Bryce embracing me outside my home is forever seared into the back of my thoughts. *"I wish you would have stayed as well."* I whisper ever so slightly in his ear.

Hoping he could hear me, and at that time his hand twitched, and it startled me. Running to call the nurse, she arrives and tells me that this is normal muscle spasms after going through so much trauma. She says, "*Most people believe it is a sign that they hear you and they are trying to let you know.*"

With a hopeful look upon her face, she reaches for my arm and squeezes it ever so slightly. She turns to leave and at that very moment I make my mind up that I can't just stay here and do nothing. It will drive me nuts. With every move or flinch that his muscles make in response to the trauma and healing process he has to go through.

I head down to the lobby and to my surprise; I see Cole coming through the sliding glass doors with that worried look upon his face. It is nice to see his face but I also can't do the drama right now. I am emotionally dragged in every direction and I am about to burst at the seams.

Struggling to keep my emotions bottled up, Cole hugs me, and I let him. Almost immediately, I feel the emotions that I have bottled up getting the better of me. I kind of push myself away and I automatically let Cole know "*I'm going to head to the office to get my mind off of the events of this morning"*

But before I could finish what I was telling him, he was scolding me about not taking the time I need to take care of myself. I know he has the best of intentions for me but man I don't need his mothering advice so he has me screaming to the top of my lungs in the parking lot, which I'm sure had everyone and their mother staring or listening to myself taking all this blame for myself. Having to explain that Bryce would not have been there if I would have just gone into work where I should have been in the first place. Or the fact that if I would've just been a big girl and spoke up and asked him to just stay the night with me, he would have already been where he was headed. A blank stare on Cole's face says it all, knowing he would do anything to help or make me understand, so I just ask him to *"just let me do this my way."* This will be the only thing that will keep me motivated.

Cole and Richard

Waiting here seems like it would be a mistake, so grabbing my things and heading to the hospital even to just be there for Jane if she may need something makes me feel like I can help in a small way. Spotting Jane as she's leaving the hospital, I hurry to get to her. I reach her and see she has tears in her eyes, which means Bryce has to be in a terrible way. Before I could ask her what is wrong and how is she doing considering the circumstances, she screams at the top of her lungs, "*Why*!" "*Why does this always happen to me?*" Not knowing how to answer this for her, I just pull her close to me and hugged her as tight as I could.

She looks at me and tells me she is going to go to the office and get right into work mode so she can give Bryce good news when he wakes up. His sister will be here tomorrow morning, so I will feel better that he won't be alone for long. I ask her if she really thinks that this is a good idea since she seems to be distraught and all over the place right now. "Maybe you should just go home and rest." I pleaded with Jane to go home and rest like she originally planned to do. But of course she responded with "*No I can't not do anything right now I feel useless and I owe Bryce.*" Confused, I asked her "*Why does she feel she owes him?*" Jane's Eyes start to well up and she responds with "*he was on his way to my house to make sure I was okay because of yesterday's events, so if it wasn't for me he wouldn't have been in that wreck in the first place.*" Now I need to meet my ride share to get back home so I can get my car. Do you have anything else to ask me? She screams with anger.

Trying to calm her down, I told her that if the accident was meant to happen it was going to happen no matter what. Wiping her tears away, she hugs me and darts for the parking lot. I hate to see her like this. I also know she is under enough stress to make a firecracker explode, so I won't push her too much.

My phone rings, and of course, it is Richard. Sometimes I wish he didn't have my number so that it would limit his bossiness and needs to only if he could find me. I answer the phone just to get this over with and Richard sounded pissed when he screamed "*now*" confused as to what I had done or if I was missing anything when I suddenly remembered that I was supposed to meet him at the clubhouse last night after our little shady mission. Boy, did he give me an ear full with such a short conversation that when he was done with his yelling. He didn't even let me respond. He just hung up.

Taking a deep breath and heading back out to my car, wondering just how much deep shit am I into, and knowing Richard, he's going to chew me up one wall and down the other and that's just the beginning. The clubhouse is an old packing warehouse with an entire upper floor renovated to the needs of the organization. The men that my father is involved with are known to make things happen and people are made to disappear, later showing up charred with no evidence to be found. Richard never really talks about the club. As long as I can remember, he's always been a part of it. Now it's my turn to join. It's made me aware of some crimes that they do and cover up. The money is a nice bonus. As long as I don't have to be the one to make a person disappear, then I'm okay.

Recalling when Richard asked me to get Jane out of her house and I asked him why he was very vague about his reasons and gave me a short response of *"If you want in, then you will make this happen. You will eventually piece it together and know what you need to and when you need to."*

I pulled up to the warehouse and two men were waiting outside the doors. If this is a sign of things to come, then I screwed up. Walking into the building, the two men the size of club bouncers follow me in with one hand on both shoulders, guiding me to my fate. They both act like robots telling me to "*follow them.*" Heading up to the loft, the elevator doors close and we begin the ascend. We come to a stop and the doors open with Richard waiting for me on the couch that surrounds a very large coffee table stacked with money and files. I know better to say anything since I'm not here on a social call, so I sit down and wait for his response.

"Cole, I asked you here last night so I could clue you into what has happened and why I asked you to get Jane out

of her house. When you didn't show, I wondered if maybe you decided you were out, so I went ahead and made other plans." Cole's face is frozen with anticipation. *"Those plans will implicate you in all of this if it goes south at any moment. So next time I call you, better not miss the conversation or the meetup. It's not only you that you have to worry about. The ramification of your actions have serious consequences because the boss is going to come down on me for it not being done efficiently and I will not pay for your mistakes. You want in? I suggest you take this seriously because it can be rewarding, but also ever so costly."*

"I'm in, I told you I want this but you're also my father I thought you would at least be honest with me and tell me why I am to deceive my friend so you could get into her home without her knowing and also following her." Even though I didn't want to know exactly why or fully agreed with Richard's motives. *"If that doesn't show you how loyal I am, then I don't know what will."*

Even after the last job, they tasked me to burn some video footage and files without asking for any information about it in return. "*So please enlighten me and I'll prove to you I'm all in."*

With a stern look on Richard's face, he slides an ominous file across the table with the demand to *"pick it up!"* flinching at the slightest movement I thrust forward to catch the file before it keeps sliding, scattering the contents on the floor. My hand slams down over the top of the file, creating a loud echo that starts in this small corner that protrudes across every inch of the room until it dissipates.

Picking it up I ask *"What is this?"*

"*Open* it!" Richard almost sounded hesitant when he impetuously answered my question.

It is a file of a man that I have only seen in photos hung on the walls around this place. "*Why am I looking at a photo of a man that was one of you?"* Richard says, *"turn to the next page and keep reading. I'll be back in a minute."* He gets up and walks to the bar across the room as I turn the page, it is a photo of a lady with light brown almost blondish hair and I have never seen her in my life so without a second guess I turn to the next page and pause for a moment as I am confused and not going to lie a little frightened it's a picture of my mother.

"What does any of this mean?"

Jane

The rideshare pulls up to my address. As I pull my thoughts and feelings together, I thank him and head inside to change my clothes and grab my things to head to Jessica's home. I walk up to my door and go to grab the handle and without effort the door opens. My pistol is upstairs in my drawer safe, so that means I have nothing to protect myself. Cautiously, I grab my phone, all the while keeping my eyes on the entryway. I dial 9-1-1. The dispatcher answers the call and asks me what the emergency is and, trying to keep my response as calm and informative as possible I relay my badge number, address and situation. She then advises me to stay put and keep an eye on the house that she is dispatching the police to my residence and to stay on the line till they get there. About five minutes later, the sirens sound in the distance, so I relay to dispatch that they are pulling up. I'm going to let them go.

Walking in behind the police as they clear the rooms one by one, *I get the immediate feeling this is not a break in and just a mistake on my part when I rushed out the door this morning to hurry and get to Bryce.* When the police officer asks me *"do you want to make a case"*, I quickly tell him "*no sir*." I might have left the door ajar in my hurry to the hospital this morning. With a smile and a handshake they all wrap it up and head out, but not without saying, *"If you need anything else, do not hesitate to call back."*

With all that being done, it sure did make me exhausted, to say the least. I watch as they get into their patrol cars and pull away before I turn to shut the door and lock it. I turn and take a deep sigh of relief when I decide to go to the kitchen and make myself a bit of food. At this point I haven't stop to eat and the effects are showing. When I leaned over and grabbed a pan out of the cabinet, I got a little dizzy and my vision went a little spotty for a quick second. Quickly grabbing the edge of the counter to brace myself from falling forward, I think to myself I need to take care of myself more. Making myself more of a priority seems to be a task I wasn't expecting. Placing my pan on the stovetop. I throw a pat of butter into the pan to make myself a hot ham and cheese sandwich with some tomato soup I throw in a saucepan. This always brings back childhood memories and makes me think of all the comforts of when I was a child and safe. Sitting at the counter with my food, time passes slowly, it seems. As I sit there and contemplate, it's been baffling the past couple of days.

Placing my bowl and plate in the sink, I headed upstairs to get dressed so I could get ready to head to the office. Bryce wants me to check in, then go to the scene of the crime that is known as Jessica's home. Boy, do I wish this was solved already. *I really needed an extended vacation.* Thoughts going through my head as I finish up getting dressed. I grab my pistol belt and head downstairs to get the rest of my files and keys that were scattered on the kitchen table. *I really need to turn my extra room into an office now that I have the space.* Slowing down just enough to make sure

I have all that I need before I lock and close the door this time, scrambling to get into my car, I cautiously pull out of the drive. *I don't want to repeat what had happened to Bryce. I need to make sure I have my head screwed on straight.*

Driving across town, I make sure I pay close attention to my surroundings and that I am on high alert for chaos. If I have learned anything about the past few days is that Karma and Destiny are playing their hands with my life and they have the royal flush. Which makes me the lucky person to be playing defense with mine. Pulling into the parking lot at work, I ran upstairs and let Blake know *"I won't be in the office today, but she could reach me on my phone if she needed anything. That I would be at Jessica's house, going over the last bit of evidence for the crime scene for my report."* She nodded and gave the signal that she heard and understood what I said, so to my office I darted. Walking over to my desk, I grab my files and computer and open my desk drawer to grab a small camera to record anything I might miss so I could have it on camera for later time if need be.

Looking around, *"I am really doing this?"* Long pause while I contemplate and I repeated myself for assurance. *"I am really doing this!"* This time, I sort of let the sound just burst out of my mouth uncontrollably.

Closing my office door and heading down the elevator, head back to the car when an alert comes across my screen that I had missed a call from a number I didn't recognize. I listened to the voicemail and it was Kelcey, Bryce's sister, telling me that *the doctors would try to bring him out of his coma today.* Hoping for good news and to show up and see him awake in the bed would be exactly what I needed. This made today that much easier to deal with.

This time when I pull up to the house, I see Cole sitting by the driveway. Wondering why he is here, I am sure with how I left things at the hospital in the lobby; he was worried about me. He slowly walks up to me and begins to plead with me to "*just go home.*"

Confused as to why he looks so pale and struggles to finish a sentence, he blurts out, "*Richard is doing shady shit and he needed to be around someone that was stable.*" Laughing out loud, I caught myself just as he scrunched up his nose to give me a serious look.

"*Cole, please explain*?"

Normally I would give my thoughts on his problems, but then remembered I shouldn't. Not because I don't want to help, but I have an obligation to report Richard of his crimes if I have the knowledge of it. So that was our agreement when we met his dad was off limits other than casual talk of family. But if a case lands him in the crosshairs because of this alleged affiliation with the mob, I would have to do my job. He knows it and I know it, so we don't talk about it.

With no response from Cole about the situation, he asks "*maybe I could go to your place and just hang out till you get off tonight?*"

"*No worries at all. Go home and make yourself comfortable. Just make sure you clean up your mess and if you leave, please shut and lock the door. I don't need another debacle like this morning.*"

Before Cole could ask, I just followed with, "*no harm no foul when you accidentally leave your door open for any and every passer-by when you're blindsided!*"

Cole Leaves and as I watch him disappear into the distance, I turn and head up the stairs to unlock the front door. Just moments before I enter the house, I decide to be just a tad bit smarter than last time and drop a pin to Blake, just in case. Then turn my phone on airplane mode so it doesn't go off later when I don't need it to.

This time I have a camera and I set it up and aim it at the tunnel but hide it so no one but me knows it is there. *Maybe, just maybe, someone or something will be caught on it and I will have the evidence I need.* Wondering if *it would be the perpetrator and if so, I could use this to nail him to the wall.*

Placing it in the dining room in a plant base, I use its natural camouflage; feeling confident that this will work. Turning to get a scope of the room, I wander over to the dining room table and pause as I glance at the floor, thinking, "*here I go again.*" Almost too hesitant to force myself to move.

I Move the rug and claw away at the recessed handle lifting the wooden door. Remembering to look at my watch, I read the time out loud in hopes there is no reason I'll be missing time when I get done down there. *Sure that this will be my last time, that I will need to go down here alone, at the very least. Hoping the next time would be to condemn the tunnel and seal it off with who they are calling "The Phantom" in restraints of his own.* Wiping my sweaty hands on my pants legs, I begin the climb down the rickety wooden ladder. Reaching the bottom of what seems like forever, my feet hit the floor with my last step and I freeze. It is colder than I remember it being the last time I was here.

Turning on my flashlight, I scan the walls and the floor for immediate signs of an intruder. Matching my feet to a set of past footprints so that I can now differentiate theirs from mine. Taking out my wallet, I place my driver's license next to one footprint for size reference and snap a picture. It is wide and deep, like the person is heavier than me. Needing more light, I remember there are lanterns along the wall. I begin to light them one by one that are within reaching distance, which makes it possible for me to notice the tank of gas and also a mask tucked around the top of it. "*I must have missed this in the dark last time?*" Snapping a photograph of the evidence, I quickly place my phone back in my pocket. The two lights give off an ominous cast of shadows that dance to their own beat. As I look down a never ending tunnel and the hesitation hits me hard.

Am I ready? Am I sure I am capable? The thoughts start to race so I try to think of something good, something calming. *I need something to quiet my mind... Bryce.* The thought of him instantly puts the angst at bay.

With nothing but shadows for as far as the eyes can see, I creep down the passageway, almost as if I am the one trying to not be detected. When that familiar thick air chokes me, causing a bitter metallic taste in the back of my throat. As that familiar smell of damp and dirty air surrounds me, it's followed by the weakening of my limbs causing me to go into Panic mode. Heaving to take in as much oxygen as I can, I see a light flicker in the distance. Out of the still, empty dark, a figure appears amongst the shadows. Grabbing my tight chest, I try to turn to run. But everything feels like it weighs a ton, causing me to stumble to the ground, tripping over my own two feet like it was the first time on them. Screaming at the top of my lungs, but nothing coming out other than a quiet but hollow gasp of air that sounded like air escaping a tire with a leak in it. My body begins to go numb and I am on all fours, slowly scrambling to think of a way to save myself this time.

This time I was ready, I grabbed my Pistol from my holster and tried to blindly aim it into the direction of the assailant in hopes of scaring him or injuring him enough that he decided that today was not the day. Feeling the Bullet leave the chamber, I hear it hit an object in the distance as it ricochets followed by someone that hollered "*You Bitch!*" knowing that if someone was to show up at the emergency room with a gun-shot wound, they will call the police. With my head feeling heavier than I can hold, I drop it like it was a twenty-pound brick, and the darkness swallows me.

This time, I am aware of what is going on around me. I feel someone picking me up, but I can't move, so to get away isn't much of an option. The walk seems like it's taking forever when he throws me down on a bed and shoves a needle into my arm that pinched and burned as whatever he put in me made its way through my system. Making that the last thing I can remember.

Waking up with a splitting headache and blurred vision, I'm a little afraid of what I find. The last place I remember being was in that passageway on a bed with a monster of a person injecting me with some sort of shit. So this view of a couch and table kind of scares me. *Is this another dream? Is this real or was I carried here?* Quickly, I sit up and look around, moving my body against the back of what seems to be a brick fireplace. *Wait, I know exactly where I am. I'm in Jessica's living room. Thinking out loud, "Now*

What? What else could possibly go wrong with this investigation?"

Looking down to check if maybe my clothes were torn or stained, I see they were not my clothes. Jumping from one thought to the next, I remember that if I was in the passageway, *maybe the camera caught the person on video?* Rushing to get to the plant with the camera that I hid beforehand, I notice that it's not there. *"What? There is no way that someone found this unless they were watching me this whole time."*

Reaching for my phone to call Cole hoping to see if he would come to the brownstone and help me, but I can't find it. Unlike last time, someone knows where I am, so I'm not completely alone in this situation. I began searching all over for the device. Shock sets in when no phone is found. In fact, no pocket at all. "*It's a dress*," I scream at the top of my lungs in sheer panic and anger. *If this person would just stop messing with me and my life, I swear I won't kill him. I'll just arrest him.* Trying to think fast but logically about what my next steps need to be, I hear someone's footsteps in the distance rustling around. Now I went from panic to determination. Quickly scurrying across the floor, trying to be as quiet as can be, I lean over to close the hatch in the floor when I yank the board to cover it quickly and I knock the chair over. *"Great Jane, now they know I'm awake and moving around." Hopefully, they were running away in sheer terror that I would catch them. At least till I come up with a plan to do this all myself.*

Out of the corner of my eye I catch a shadow flicker coming up behind me and with one fell swoop he knocks me over the head, making me fall to the floor on my stomach. This masked man grabs me by my ankle and starts to drag me towards the living room when I kick myself free. Getting up to run across the room pretty damn quickly to get to the front door, I cut the corner and stumbled as the rug slipped out from underneath me. Glancing behind me to see where he was and not seeing him, I turn back to see my clear path to freedom when I notice the door being blocked by a hutch that should have been against the wall. Compelling myself to turn around, I am aggressively greeted by this man and his fist; he knocks me back first into the hutch, then onto the floor. *God, I am so sick of taking people's punches!* So I attempt to deliver a few blows of my own, but they don't seem to pack the punch they need to. I am this little old five foot two woman that probably only weighs a hundred and twenty pounds soaking wet. He is a six-foot man that seems to know what he is doing, considering he seems to have the same motive as the last attack.

This tall and muscular man grabs my hand as I withdraw a punch to his face and jerks me around. Forcing both hands down to my side and picking me up to carry me back to the living room. *Expecting this outcome to be any different from the last encounter would be downright foolish of me. So collecting as much information as possible would be the best thing for me when I get out of this mess.* He dropped me to the floor as fast as someone dropping a hot plate handed to them without oven gloves and lifted his foot and inserted it into my side. One blow at a time followed one after another and about one too many. I spat up some blood. That taste of iron and the radiating pain from what might be my ribs broken, or a punctured organ, I cry out "***STOP!***" over and over in between the gasp of air. Turning over onto my stomach to relieve my abdomen from being the target, I notice the fire poker laying next to me on the ground. Trying to figure a way out of this, I lay as still as possible so that he would stop, thinking that I might have passed out from all the pain and beatings he had laid upon me.

He stops! I can't believe it actually worked. Laying there on the hard cold surface that is partially covered with an old rug, I try to listen for the sounds of what this man's next moves will be. Terror seeps into every crevice of my body, waiting for the unknown of what might happen next. *I'm going to die and there is nothing I can do to stop it. Knowing that Jessica dies in this very room in this very spot sends chills coursing through my veins.* This is it, I thought. *Now is the time that I stand for these women and make their stories worth dying for.*

Sliding closer to the fire pit inch by inch to get the fire poker so that it will be within reaching distance to defend myself. I hear a drawer slam shut and a voice holler, "*where is it?*" Pausing in sheer fright as to what he is talking about, I hear his footsteps coming closer with rage. Trying to pay attention to how close he got, I was prepared to swing the weapon that I just procured at him to try and get away and hide. But he has one on me. He flipped the coffee table over on top of me, trapping me under it as I turned over to hit him, causing the weapon to fall from my grip, pinning my arms under it. The poker stabbing me in the rib with the small curved barb as he puts pressure on the table. With both the table and him on top of me, he puts a lamp cord against my throat, hollering, "*where is the proof?*"

I will kill you then find it, but if you just tell me, I will make it quick instead of torturing you to get it, but don't mistake me for caring. I am only doing this because they ordered me to. I don't give a shit about your crying or pleading.

Bryce

Feeling my fingers move oh so slowly but more on the twitchy side, kind of like the twitches out of a SyFy horror film, I think to myself, why does it hurt so much to move them and why is something attached to my finger? Listening to the sounds and ruckus surrounding me, I hear a familiar voice. It's Kelcey, my sister, and I can hear her talking to another person about me. Trying to open my eyes, everything in sight is a blur. I can hear Kelcey ask him, “is my brother going to be okay?” The doctor responds with, “we will only know when the medicine brings him fully out of the coma and he wakes up so we can do assessments on him." With that said, I move around just a little, guessing that they notice my movement and Kelcey suddenly runs to my side from the foot of the bed. Grabbing my hand she asks "can you hear me?" Not able to respond because of the mask on my face and being groggy, I just squeezed her hand for acknowledgement. "Bryce," the doctor asks with a low, calm voice, "are you in a lot of pain? If so, squeeze Kelceys hand." Focusing my vision a bit more, I can see her face beaming in on me in hopes of a good response. I manage to get out a small grunt with a nod. The doctor turns to leave as he tells Kelcey and I that *"he will be back with the nurses and some medication that I need to relax and stay calm."* Feeling exhausted already, I try to readjust in bed and make myself more comfortable, but that does nothing but make me wince in pain. Kelcey grabs the chair and pulls it as close to the bedside as possible and asks "*if she could do anything or call anyone?"* I just look at her and reach for the oxygen mask that is on my face to pull it down and I whisper, "*Jane*."

Laying there waiting on the doctor to return, the nurse knocks on the door and brings in a mix of concoctions, one in a syringe and in the other hand some water in a cup. She distributes the medicine and I feel my body increasingly becoming warm and relaxed. She leans in and tells me, "*she's going to collect some blood samples while she is here to run the necessary tests for the doctor.*"

Knowing that the medicine is working, I tell Kelcey, "*Jane would want to know.*" Kelcey tells me, "*She was here yesterday the whole day waiting for you to get out of surgery.*"

Pour Jane, I bet she is worried about me. This whole mess of a situation would take a toll on anyone.

With all the medications kicking in, I get drowsy and start nodding off. The feeling of being relaxed has me drifting into a vivid and lucid dream.

There is a knock at the door and I get up from my desk, frustrated, wondering why my assistant didn't let me know someone was coming to see me. I quickly open the door to my office and it is Jane standing there in a trench coat and heels with her hair done in such a way I haven't seen. Her eyes are painted in a smokey manner with golds and blacks that make her green eyes radiate so emerald green you could almost not see past them. *They are hunting in the most seductive way.* With a slight flush of red on her cheeks and her pouty lips just ever so slightly ajar, she places her hand next to her hair and tucks the wavy curls away from her face.

Thanking to myself *she is such a beautiful and brilliant woman and all I want to do is make her mine.* She leans close to me and places her hand on my chest so softly that it makes my body shiver with chills.

I ask her "*what she was doing here at the office all dressed up and her response to me was, it's date night.*"

"Boy, did I miss something? Did I bump my head? Am I sick?"

With that being said, Jane steps through the door and seductively says, "*Where are you taking me, or did you forget?*"

Not that I didn't want this. I was just so lost and confused as to what was going on she said *"just kidding*".

With an even more confused look upon my face, I wanted to ask what she meant by that if she was here? Before I could ask her, she acknowledged the look on my face and said, "*I am just kidding because they were staying here!*" With my heart beating in my chest and my palms beginning to sweat, she slowly unbuttons herself.

Taking her coat off in a sexy manner, she leans in as close as possible behind me and whispers the safe word is "*Toxic.*"

Now my heart is beating out of my chest as Jane runs her hand down my arm and spins me around. I am face to face with her and I can smell her perfume. *She is so intoxicating it makes me want to take her now to sink my teeth into her soft and supple body.* She shoves me into the chair and raises her dress just ever so slightly, making it easy to lift her leg and straddle me. Not able to control myself and without a thought, I grab the back of her head and tug her closer to my face, leaving my fingers entangled in her hair.

Taking in the sight and smells of her, I hesitate to make a mistake by rushing this moment. But with no forethought about any repercussions of my actions, I kiss her. Her warm lips are so moist and plump it makes it hard not to bite her. Jane moves her hands down the buttons of my shirt and makes her way to my belt. Making haste with the belt buckle. She yanks the belt out of my jeans with a swift, steady motion and wraps it around her neck, wearing it like a scarf, leaving her hands free. "keeping it close for later" she winks.

She moves on to the button and zipper, getting the material out of the way.

In my mind, not knowing if I could handle the intensity of the moment, I picked her up, grabbing her waist with both hands, and she wrapped her warm thighs around me. Thinking of this woman and what I have only long for, for so long. Turning to sit her on the desk she says "*now get down on your knees*" with no hesitation I drop to the floor and she picks her foot up and sits it on the innermost part of my shoulder where my beard is rubbing up against her smooth legs.

"*That's my good boy,"* she growls. Her demand gave me a grin I thought I would never have had but I like what she is doing to me.

The view from this perspective is one I needed the light down low, with a subtle ambiance that outlines every line of Jane's figure. Kissing her leg, working my way up to her inner thigh, she shakes from chills and closes her legs around my head along with both of her hands full of my hair. Forcing me to pause. Watching her reaction is so intoxicating as she relaxes, allowing me to take my mouth and caress her hot, wet body. Watching her squirm and moan as she arches her back and climaxes makes my cock throb.

Wiping away the cum off my mouth, my hands work their way to where my mouth just left. *I want to watch her enjoy this.* Entering her body with my fingers, I slowly work them in a thrusting manner, in and out in a waving motion. Her body begging for more, beginning to violently shake, I cup her pussy with my mouth to send her over the edge. Jane hollers uncontrollably *"no!"* I pause for just a moment and she gets up and turns around, "unzip me."

Now it is time to take it slow and tease her in the same way she started with me, just she doesn't know I have wanted this for so long that I have the patience for it. I grab her hair around the base of her neck and slide it to one side, making it easier to unzip her dress and passionately kiss her on the neck. Pulling the zipper slowly down, I expose her bare skin, revealing itself causing my cock to pulse even harder. I bend her over the desk and lean forward to run my lips down her back as my hands unclasp her bra. Watching her body squirm makes the male instinct in me take over as I gently scratch her back. Her breath gradually gets deeper. Knowing the torture I am putting her through makes this slow trot to the finish line so worth the wait.

Stepping back just a second before taking in her body, Jane turns to see why I stopped. The sultry smile on her face shows excitement that burns through my soul for her.

She says *"Good daddy, now don't stop."*

Responding, "*I am going to make you beg me to keep going.*"

"*Now turn back around and take it like a good girl.*"

Through the dimly lit room, I can see the fire ignite in her eyes as she smiles and turns around. Slowly leaning across the desk with her dramatic response "*is this how you want me?*"

With her bent over, I interlace my fingers into hers, pressing my cock against her round and supple ass. Grabbing my belt from around her neck, I slide the cold leather around her waist, using it as an anchor. Watching the belt tighten around her supple hips, she braces herself against the hardwood desk.

Gripping my cock in my hand and stroking it oh so slightly as it gets harder, I slide the tip of the head into Jane's warm and soft body. I can feel her body pulse around my penis, causing me to fight the urge to just ride her hard and put her up wet. Listening to her moan as she bares down on my cock, feeding her pussy every inch of me and she wants more. Turning me on to the point I might not make it to the end of this round. Stopping everything biding my time, I pull out and turn Jane over; I push her on her back so I can watch her face. Jane closes her eyes and smiles at the same time as she is biting her bottom lip. My hands making their way up Jane's body and cupping both of her breasts in my hands, taking it all in. She knows exactly what she is doing to me. I only hesitate for a brief moment before I grab Jane around the throat with a slight playful squeeze and force my cock into her, watching her bite her lip even harder and enjoy it all. I can feel the cum running down her inner thigh as I take what I want from her body. I lifted her leg up onto my shoulder and thrust in an aggressive manner, to which we almost knocked over the lamp and computer on my desk. Jane screams louder and louder the rougher we get. I grab hold of the belt to give me more control of the motion, but it seems to not be enough as she digs in her nails into my arms. Almost folding her in half with her leg over my head, I lean down, not stopping the pounding I was giving her, and take one of her nipples in my mouth. She finally grabs with both of her hands my hair and squeezes my head in her hands as she bares down on my body with her thighs. Jane's body shakes as warm white wet cum oozes out of her onto my hard sheath. Not being able to contain myself listening to her scream my name, I pound her harder and faster, just in time I pull out and let myself drip all down her chest.

Knock at the office door rushes us along with both of us being startled by the knock on the door. We rush to gather our clothes and to throw them on when I hear my sister Kelcey holler for me. *That is strange because the last time I knew she lived in Texas.* Shouting to "*wait a minute*" I feel as though someone is shaking me and I wake up.

Kelcey was leaning over me with a worried look upon her face and telling me I was talking out loud, that I was saying some unsavory things for a sister's ears. In a cold sweat and wide eyed, I now realize that, that amazing situation was just me dreaming. *Maybe it was because of the drugs they used to make me relax, mixed with feeling little to no pain. All I know is when can I go back to sleep and do it again.*

Octavia C. Penn

Kelcey butts in and tells me the Doctor said "*all the labs are good and they will be around to take him for some follow-up test tomorrow morning and a cat scan to see how his brain is doing if all is well I will go home at the end of the week.*"

COLE AND RICHARD

Glaring at the page for what seemed forever I hear in the distance "*Turn the page and keep digging!*" Raising my head in an angry manner looking at Richard with eyes that could kill, I slowly turn the page not knowing what I am going to find. So far all I have seen are three photos: one of my mother, one of a man that is no longer a member of this club and organization, much less he's not even alive for what he did to it. That speaks volumes in my mind about what kind of man he was and one of a random lady I did not even recognize. As I am trying to turn to the next page, my fingers refuse to grasp the edges to separate, as if I need to add a bit of spit to them to help grip the page. The next page is my birth certificate, not sure why Richard has a file on me considering he knows me pretty well. I would say, considering he is my father? But what father, even one that is connected to the mob and all its shadiness, would threaten or blackmail his own son? *Really? Who would do something like that?* Richard hollers from across the warehouse to ask me if I would like a stiff drink to go with the news of what I am reading. Looking back up in his direction, I just shout out, "*water is fine!*" Still not sure why I am looking at this, I continue to scan the page, but noticing something out of place. On my birth certificate, it has my mother's name as Jessica White and my paternal father as AJ White. Why does this piece of paper have the man on the front page listed as my father and a woman I have never in my life or laid eyes on listed as my mother? Confused as to where this is leading, I continue to think, think about my whole life as far back as I could remember. I can't for the life of me remember anything before I was about three years old. Glancing up at Richard, I see a smirk on his face. That man's name is AJ White. I pause for a second and realize that, that name is looking and sounding quite familiar. For one, the last name White, is the same as the lady that was found dead on her living room floor a few days ago. Unsure, but now I know something is wrong. Richard is trying to rattle me into doing as he wishes, no matter the cost. That has got to be what this is. I knew at some point down the road I was going to be involved in some shady shit, but I thought it would at least be later rather than sooner. "*Richard, you better tell me what this is!*"

Richard makes his way over to the couch across from me and takes a seat. Leaning forward to place the water on a coaster in front of me, he then sits back and crosses his legs. With that dangerous glare that he is beaming in my direction, I dare ask, "*What is this pile of crap that I am holding on to?*" Staring each other down, there is an awkward silence among us. And with a slow hand, Richard places his drink to his lips and takes a guzzle of the bourbon he just sat down with. "*Now, Richard says, do I have your attention?*" nodding at my response, he says, now that you read the information on the page I am going to clue you in on something that will change your life, and I'm going to need you to put on your big boy pants and get over it.

This has got to be something major because I have never seen Richard this serious about anything about my mother or myself.

I chime in, "*real quick before you say anything. What does this other woman and AJ have to do with my mother or me?"*

"Cole, if you could just shut up for a moment, I would have the time to tell you!"

"*Okay, Richard, you have my attention."*

"Good, because when I tell you what I am about to, it is going to change the course of your life from here on out."

Worried about what bad revelation Richard is about to lay on me, I brace myself. Richard then lays the events of a timeline out for me that doesn't seem to play out the way I assumed it did.

"Cole, when you were born, the circumstances that surrounded your birth are Skewed from what we told you happened. Your mother's name is actually Jessica White and your father is AJ White." About three…

"Wait, you can't just say that and move on! Much less think I am going to believe this shit!"

"*Well, if you would let me finish, you would know that I have your DNA test from when you, your father and your mother when you were discharged from the hospital two days later. And like I said, keep reading and turn the page you might understand when I'm done."*

Sitting back, I open the file and continue reading as Richard continues with this information overload. He continues with the recounts of the night I was born. Richard then tells me "*Jessica was Pregnant with me and with her losing her first-born child to a tragedy that she never spoke of and never wanted another child which in turn made AJ try to give you away to anyone who would take you."*

"*Jessica's only request was that you go to a loving family, and that you stayed close enough. She could make sure you were taken care of till she was sure you were okay."*

"*Well, at that time AJ and I were club members and good friends and my wife, also the woman that raised you and loved you. She couldn't have kids because of the cancer and treatments she had to endure. Your mother loved you unconditionally from the moment that I got you from AJ and placed you in her arms."* I feel my heart break into a million pieces when I think of my loving mother.

"*She always said you were her little miracle and if I could have I would have given my life for hers so she could have been a mother longer. So please don't change how you feel about her. We wanted you and loved you like our own."*

Sitting there with a blank stare on my face looking at Richard, thinking to myself, *that is why I never saw myself looking like either one of them. I just thought I looked like someone else from our family tree.* Richard snaps his fingers and asks me, *"could I get you something other than the water you are drinking now that you have had time to process some of the information?"*

"Whiskey neat," I gruffed.

Before that sentence was complete, I realized and jerked my head in his direction and said, "*Some of the information*?"

He just gets up and walks away and leaves me with that thought in my head! *How am I supposed to process all of this and be okay with it? What else does he have to say?*

Standing in front of me, Richard hands me a glass and sits back down, but this time next to me. "*Okay, quit dragging this out. What is the rest of this information?"*

Tensions rise as we sit there and Richard lets my imagination run wild. Richard takes another drink and settles back into his chair. "*With the information I just gave you, I need you to understand where we stand as of now. Not who or what you were born into. Our agreement still stands that we agreed upon when this whole scenario started. Agree?"*

I hesitated for a second, but if I agreed, there was no backing out. *How could I, now that I have this file with unearthed information about my true past?*

"Yes, I agree."

Okay, now let's get down to the main business that I brought you here for. Now that you know that your birth mother is Jessica and AJ is your father, I need you to know that the sibling that you have is alive. The baby did not die at birth in a tragedy, as AJ told his wife.

"See, AJ was in deep with some terrible people and they made him take a deal and if he didn't, it was going to cost him his life dearly." My eyes widen as the truth unravels.

How could someone do that to a person they say they love?

Anger starts to fuel my rage and I just shout, "***GOOD****! Anyone who does that to another person should rot in hell where they belong."* Richard shakes his head in approval; he just continues.

"See, there were a few of us that knew what was going on and we all pulled together to try and help Jessica and AJ out, but he just wouldn't take it. He was convinced that he could do it all on his own. But when Jessica had you, she had started to bleed out, and they had to rush her into emergency surgery, never getting to see or hold her own child."

"That is when AJ concocted this scheme to take the baby and sell her to someone who was willing to pay him a large lump sum of money for his problems. Now my wife and I also have been trying for years to conceive a child of our own and the doctors told us that it wasn't going to be possible with her cancer diagnosis. So, trying to give your mom a child to love as her own and give her, her dying wish; we emptied our savings and 401 account and gave it all to AJ."

"I still don't understand. What does this have to do with our agreement? Me helping you get information on Jane?"

Jane

With the lamp cord pressed against my throat and the fire poker stabbing against my rib, my first thought is to think of something to get him off of me.

As he screams in a deep, dark and aggressive growl, "*Where the Fuck is the key? You won't have long to give me what I want before I take it myself!*"

Fear in my eyes, I struggle to turn my head toward the dining room. I attempt to plead with him as I choke on the lack of air that is allowed to fill my lungs. Trying to get the words out "*upstairs*" is all I could mutter out with sound while he was strangling me. I tried pleading with him that it was in the bottom dresser upstairs in the bedroom as best I could. But no use as long as the cord was pressed down against my neck. With the motion of my eyes and slight tilt of my head, it forces him to let off of my throat just enough. My intentions were to get him to get up and get some distance between us to help give me an upper hand, but as he lifts the cord off my

throat, he then throws the lamp across the room, shattering it into a million pieces. Flinching at the sudden aggressive noise and movement, he flips me over. Beginning to panic as I scramble trying to grab the fire poker, failing to get an actual grip on it, he hits me first in the face then wherever he seems to land his blows. Restraining me by zip tying my hands behind my back. He then takes a handful of my hair and begins to drag me with him to the stairway out of the living room and through the dining room. The thoughts of how this man has the same motive with women and the patterns repeat themselves. With each room he drags me through, there is a different level of fear and panic. Going from a rug and hardwood floor to my side catching the transition in the doorway and squishing more blood out, leaving a blood stain trail to the tile in the dining room. To the smell of the different chemicals that were used to clean the floors of Jessica's house.

This time, he stops at the bottom of the stairway and turns to look at me. He kneels down and gets right next to my ear with one hand pushing on my chest and whispers in a low growl, "*Be still and don't make a sound. I will be back. I suggest you don't press your luck with me. I am not the patient kind.*"

The notion of him climbing the stairs one heavy foot after another only to find nothing in the dresser and coming back down to kill me gives me the motivation to try and stand to run. Thanking to myself, "*Okay Jane, get it together and find a way to get yourself out of this.*" With me flipped over I Scrunch my body like an inchworm to get my knees up under myself. Wincing with every move, as it is a struggle to even attempt it. *Time seems to never be on my side.* In the amount of pain I am currently in, I am crying and bleeding out with every breath and movement that I make. I can hear that man yanking out the dresser drawers like it is nothing but a one pound piece of wood and dumping everything on the floor. The thuds echo down the stairway when he throws the drawer to move on to the next. Trying again to get up, I get one of my legs under me as I push my head against the wall to stop myself from sliding.

This time I hear him throw something against the mirror and it shatters and he hollers, "*Where is the fucking key?*"

Now, with me being able to get both legs under me and stooping over, I quickly climb to my feet to turn and run. With the light glistening in from the window blinding me, I see something shining out the corner of a picture frame thinking *what are the odds that this happens at this very moment.* With the back door in sight, I make a beeline for it, only to lose my footing and fall over my own puddle of blood. Hitting the corner of my head on a small table on the way out of the house. Everything goes dark for the moment, but I can still hear the chaos in the upstairs bedroom. *Come on, Jane, stop being clumsy.*

Hearing a door slam shut and the man barrel down the stairs, he hollers, "*You Stupid Bitch*" as he punches a hole in the wall out of anger.

That's it, thinking *the more I piss him off, the more trail he leaves behind and I will eventually catch him.*

Octavia C. Penn

He grabs me by the feet and drags me back to the living room through my blood, leaving me on the floor. Pulling out a gun he holds it on me while I then watch him grab his phone and start dialing a number.

"*It's me. What do you want me to do? She won't tell me where the key is?*" After a lengthy call he hangs up.

I know that voice? I have heard it before.

Thinking *this is it. That man just gave me a major clue to follow when he spoke in his normal voice.* Trying to hold on to the sound that he gave me, my mind tries to pinpoint where I have heard it from.

He hovers over me and takes a knife out of his pocket then says "*I'm going to cut the zip ties off and you're going to lead me to the key. I am going to get those documents one way or another.*" Yanking me to one side and forcefully cutting through the bloody plastic, he says, "*show me or there will be consequences.*"

Grabbing the fire poker and swinging it sadistically at him, I wound him in the shoulder. Trying to yank at the mask he was wearing to uncover his face, but he was just out of reach, he quickly pulled the pistol from his waistband and pointed it at my head. "*Your luck is about to run out and you're trying my patience! Tell me where the key is, or it's over and I will do this on my own. Either way, I am getting what I came here for.*"

A knock on the door startles him, and I scream for help. Stepping in and throwing his hand around my mouth, he hushes me with the threat of the gun at my temple. The knock continues one knock at a time. A man hollers "*Mrs. White, I heard some ruckus and wanted to make sure you are home and okay?*" At that time, praying with all I have that the commotion that they heard would help me. That they would send for help? It seemed like forever went by and nothing happened. Then the footsteps led away, and it was just me, helpless, once again.

We were both standing in the dark but both wanting two very different outcomes and at that moment he takes his knife against my throat and slid it from one side to the other. With both hands, I grab my neck, wrapping them as tight as I could. Blood seeping down my throat and staining the clothes from a pale blue to a deep dark red. My knees hit the ground and all I could do was pray for mercy that this would be over quickly. This man has the audacity to stoop over in front of me and tells me to "*Just die Bitch the headache isn't worth it.*"

Tears running down my face, and with eminence fear and restraint I don't want to give him the satisfaction of showing any fear or emotional response to his sadistic behavior. He turns and leaves the room, leaving me on the floor alone, bleeding out with my heart breaking and hurting for Jessica. No person should ever have to endure this brutal torture and now the end is near. She has to die alone in a room with no one that cares, like this.

The room is fading in and out to black, as I am beginning to drift off and with sounds that begin to fade and be muffled. Time is beginning to slow down and everything feels heavy. I feel the pounding on the floor as the man approaches me one more time. He forces me over face down and uses the zip ties once again to put my hands back together.

Knowing what's next will be the moment my heart will stop and I will cease to exist for this one moment as Jessica. Hearing the click and the cold hard barrel press against the back of my head, I let my last breath of air go and

I am gone with the crack of sound that fills the room that echoes into my memories.

It's dark and damp on the floor. This is exactly where I was when I slipped through time at the beginning of this day. Sliding my body against the floor to brace myself against the wall. The aftermath of what torment I just experienced has broken me. Head falling, tilted over into my arms that I desperately wrap around my legs clutching them, I just begin sobbing. Second guessing my ability to solve any of this has me too paralyzed to move. Wondering what time it was and how long I was gone.

Thinking *I need to get out of here.*

About to get up, I hear footsteps coming from the distance at a speedy pace. This time they aren't running away, they are coming towards me. This dark figure coming from the opposite end of this long shadow filled cavity has all the sounds echoing from one wall to the other. Wishing I could close my eyes and just disappear into the darkness, I began to holler as I reached for my pistol as the rush of adrenaline began to kick in.

"Stop, I'll shoot you!,"

"Stop, I mean it!"

Octavia C. Penn

"Don't come any closer!
I am warning you, I will do it!"

"You won't do shit," the voice says, coming from the shadowed figure barreling down the dark abyss.

Hands shaking uncontrollably, I cock the hammer down on my pistol and bellow out "*watch me*" before firing off a round into his abdomen. He then hits the ground like a ton of bricks. First dropping to his knees, holding on to his gut, slowly followed by collapsing to both of his hands. I can see the blood trickle down onto the surrounding ground with a horrifying sound of him gasping for air. Reluctantly walking over to unmask the man that has been terrorizing me and murdering multiple innocent women for the past two weeks. I desperately want to put a stop to his terror, so I reach down to yank the mask off his beady little head.

He yells out "***NO***" but this time it sounded scared, not with anger coming from his voice like earlier. I wasn't expecting to be shell-shocked as I pulled off the mask. I can't believe my eyes. They widen and focus in on the person I was getting ready to kill with my pistol for coming after me stumbling backwards into the wall, so confused *it's, it's Cole? What? Why? I don't understand what is going on?*

Octavia C. Penn

At this very moment, nothing is making any sense. *Why would Cole be in this tunnel and coming after me like this?*

"Cole, what the hell are you doing?"

"No excuses from you. Why are you doing this?" Answer me now!

"After what I just witnessed and went through, I deserve an answer. You were coming after me like a lunatic with his head not screwed on right."

Cole's blank stare into my soul was unfeeling and cut through me like ice, like it wasn't him responsible for what he just attempted.

Cole responded while heaving in pain. *"You will never understand why I am here! Besides, I tried to tell you earlier, and you didn't want any part of it. You brushed me off like I was an inconvenience to you. So as far as I am concerned I owe you nothing and you have it coming."*

Even more confused now than before, his vague response to my question I take a quick second to react to him jumping to his feet and lunging towards me. Reacting to the motion, I shoved him to one side and back to the floor. Just this time, it wasn't a controlled fall and his face slammed into the brick. His eyes darken and with a low growl he says to me, "*you have always had it made and nothing ever goes my way!"*

"Cole, I don't get it. You have your job, your father and me. Why are you trying to put this on me?" I ask as my blood pressure rises with my anger. *"You know what? Fuck this, you're coming with me to the station!"*

As I reach down to grab him, he swings his arm upward across his body, striking my face and knocking me back off my feet and onto my ass. Thinking *that is the last time some "Boy" is going to hit me.* Standing quickly before he could make it to his feet, I threw my knee in an upward motion, connecting with his face to knock him back. "*I'm going to be the one to do the dragging this time,"* I scream.

I am beyond tired of being the victim in the scenarios. It's just crazy that this is supposed to be my best friend and now he is trying to kill me.

"*Who sent you?"* I demanded.

Bryce

With my recovery going so well, Kelcey prepares to go back home and on with her life. The time spent with her these past few days has meant the world to me. Ever since we graduated high school and moved on to bigger and better things we wanted in our lives, we kind of lost touch with each other. Other than the usual holidays or casual phone calls. It makes me miss my family that much more. Gathering her belongings and giving me her goodbye speech makes me see our mother in her demeanor. It's good to see her doing well for herself. Giving me a hug and a kiss on the cheek, she says goodbye one final time.

It only takes about an hour after she leaves for me to get antsy going out of my mind with all the quiet in this room. Thinking about all the things in the office that need my attention and the deadlines that are quickly approaching have my nerves in knots, so I pick up my phone and call the office. My assistant picks up, and it is like business as usual. She opens with *"Mr.Gambles office. Blake, it's me Bryce. Just listen and follow my instructions to the letter when we get off the phone."* With the other end of the phone at a dead silence, the conversation only lasts about 30 seconds and we are done.

The door opens at the exact same time a knock interrupts me, trying to plot my escape from this white coat circus. It is just the nurse coming for her usual rounds of torture.

"Need to drain my body of its precious blood today?"

I should start charging y'all for this. I feel like it is now considered donations at this point.

She smiles and with a quick and witty response, she replies with, *"Nope, I am going to need you to undress and to step into my office."*

Pointing toward the Bathroom she then turns to drag in a cart with sponges, soaps and gauze of the medical kind.

"I see, and I thought you were my friend."

With a smile on my face, knowing damn well she probably loathes this, I turn and try to attempt a strut to the shower in all my glory.

"It's nice to know you can still move at your age," she smirks, *"what are you, 50?"*

"Hey, that's not called for. I'm only forty-five, for a matter of fact." Guess it doesn't help with all my gray hair that has already taken place on this head of mine.

With all the fun and games over with, she washes all the wounds and quickly follows it with the medication and carefully dressing them. Let me tell you, that shit is painful. After washing it and getting all the gunk out of the crevices, it was almost like a fresh wound. Just having to bathe and then dress in a medical gown and attempt to climb back into bed with my ass hanging out has taken its toll on me. I am more than ready to go to sleep. No meds needed.

The nurse turns off the light and says *"Sweet dreams grandpa"* and closes the door as she leaves the room "*There now I can relax"* as I say it out loud hoping she hears me as she shuts the door behind her *"grandpa my ass."*

"Good, that has been taken care of, I can now focus on other matters at hand." Searching for my phone that I somehow misplaced in this bed seems to be a task that I can't seem to keep on top of at the moment. Taking the sheets and the top cover off one end of the bed that I was currently sitting under, I created what resembles a mushroom cloud when I throw them up like a parachute in the air and snap them back down. Leaving me in this quiet room to hear this horrid drop on the tile floor. Worried that the sound was my phone and that I might have lost the only communication to the outside world, I reached down and picked it up off the ground. A small crack on the screen but it seems everything can still work, so I open my messages and begin to send a quick text to Jane.

"Jane, it is Bryce. I heard that you were here when I was brought in on a life flight, but I haven't heard from you since then. I just wanted to hear your voice and to make sure you're doing okay. Also wanted to check and see where you were on the Jessica case. If you could call me and let me know how you are, it would ease my mind a bit."

Setting my phone down on my lap, I tilt my head back to rest it on the pillow, I feel myself drifting off. Just as every muscle went asleep from being so relaxed and being clean with the help of the pain medicine, I think about Jane as I start to dose. What I want to tell her when we see each other again. Perking right up, I pick the phone up and send her a quick message.

"It would be nice to see you when you're done doing what you are taking care of. There is something that I would like to tell you in person. Just get back with me when you get this, please, Bryce."

Hours pass and no response from Jane at this point. Looking at the messages, I see she hasn't received them. A knock on my room door echos in this quiet room of mine. *"Come in"* It is Blake, my assistant. *"Good, now that you are here, I need you to catch me up on all of the case files so I can finish everything for when I return tomorrow."* She tosses me a briefcase that typically holds my files and smirks. I won't be able to do much, but at least I could go to the office and do all the paperwork from there. I need to feel productive.

"On another note, have you seen or spoken to Jane?" Blake looks confused as to what I am talking about. With a

slow but concerned look upon her face, she responds, *"She came to the office and left almost immediately. She told me to call her if I needed anything, but I haven't needed her today. Why? What do you need? She was going to that house to finish up the investigation, is what she told me."*

Picking up my phone I call again and just like last time I get her voicemail not waiting to leave on I just hang up and fling the covers off of me. *"What are you doing?"* Blake screeches with her high-pitched voice.

"Okay, enough is enough. I am leaving now. I need you to get the nurse so I can get out of this place. You can't miss her. She is the one with a smart mouth and quick response." Blake looks at me puzzled and says, *"meet your match?"* With a quick side eye, she turns to get the nurse.

The only thing racing through my mind is *that last time I couldn't get a hold of Jane. What if something happened to her? I still don't know what it was. What if something happened to her and no one's any the wiser? Hoping that she comes quickly with discharge papers or I am going to up and sneak out, leaving Blake to deal with the hospital and their AMA paperwork.*

Going about as fast as an old man with a cane that can move, I attempt to locate and dress myself with actual clothes. Seeing how well that happened last time, and that was with help and no pants. *I don't see this going quick considering that I am no James Bond or MacGyver. I sure as hell am not asking Blake to help me. That poor girl is young enough to be my daughter. I would scar her for life.*

One foot at a time, I attempt to put one foot into my jeans and fall over towards the bed to catch myself. *"Damn, get my ass in gear and get my shit together"* putting my other foot in while I am forced to lean on the bed, I pull the pants up and button them.

Next is my shirt, *see as how I hold most of my injuries in my upper chest. I might just leave shirtless.*

I can't even get the hospital gown on without wanting to cry. Fuck it shirtless, it is.

Getting the rest of my belongings gathered together, Blake comes back through the door. But this time it isn't just her. She brought the hag back with her.

"*Mr. Gamble, if you are determined to run away, then I will need your John Hancock right here."*

Pointing at the paper on a clipboard. Handing it to me, I see a paper folded in half and a pen guessing it is to sign my release papers with. She quickly mumbles low and slow, "*the paper is your prescription and if you need anything else, just give me a call personally.*"

She backs away and grabs the board out of my hands, leaving the folded paper in my hand with a manila folder *"have a great day as she closes the room."* A little embarrassed, oh how she acted in front of Blake. I open the paper and it reads, *Call for a good time, Ashley.*

Blake said, *"You going to call her?"*

"How did you know that it was her number on the paper?"

"Well, I might be young, but I am not dumb. I see and hear more than what people think I do. When I went to the nurses' desk, that nurse and two other ladies were giggling about something to do with your gown not being tied shut, so she saw your ass and all its glory when you were shaking it like an old man." I would figure as she kinda smirks, like she is making fun of me.

"So, are you going to call her? Or tell Jane about her?"

With a quick turn of my head, I look at Blake and tell her, *"it is none of your business, but no I'm not!"*

"Not tell her or not Call her?"

"For Christ's sake, Blake, grab the files and let's get out of here. I feel like I am talking to a child about something that I shouldn't be." Running out of the room and passing the nurses' desk, my face draws flush with embarrassment. We make it to the sliding entrance doors and I come to a halt like a car that just hit a brick wall. *"Really? Of all the circumstances we leave this place, it's doing the same thing outside as it was when it put me in this place!"*

"Blake, you're driving,"

She looks at me and says, *"You bet your ass I am. I don't want to be in this place like you, with the way you drive."* With her sassy walk to the enormous hummer that she drives, wondering how she maneuvers it in these small streets. Asking her why she drives such a big vehicle. Being such a petite girl, she comes back with, *"It's big enough to protect me if something were to happen like it did you. At least that is what my father said to me."* Nodding regarding her father for trying to keep his little girl safe, I can understand why. *"Come on, let's get you to the office old man,"* Blake barks her demands towards me.

Cole and Richard

"Jane is the missing link in this whole chain we are carrying around on our backs and before we go any further, I need to tell you that this is all coming down the line from higher up."

Silent stare in Richards' direction and I can't help but wonder what else is going to spill out of his mouth.

"Now that they all found out what happened, they are tying loose ends up and I am the one they are forcing to carry it all out since I was smack in the middle of it all. I will protect you for as long as possible, but I need you to know you and me are all that matter as of now. Not friends or acquaintances."

"Okay," Coles' aggressive replies. Sounding almost hateful towards Richard.

Taking a deep breath, he continues, "*Jane is the child that was passed around through the black market in exchange for money that ended up eventually killing her father. Hell, your birth father if you wanted to get technical. So that makes Jane your biological sister. And the job that we did last week has everything to do with you and your sister."*

Cole interrupts with a burst of anger."*I can't believe you! You knew this whole time and instead of telling me so I could get to know my sister. I was stuck helping you!"*

That is the reason I had you get close to your sister! Richard slams his hand down on the table!

"*Because of the money that the organization is looking to get back with interest on a bad deal that AJ screwed over on them. On you and your sister!"*

Richard gets up, walking from one side of the table to make his way around to my side. The look on his face doesn't match the tone in his voice as he tells me he did all of this for me.

"I'm done with your excuses, Richard!"

"Would you just shut your trap and listen? You will understand when I finish telling you what happened and why I never told you about Jane or hell, your birth parents."

"AJ died while he was going to meet an associate in the warehouse district. But what he didn't know is it was all a setup and the person he was meeting was a plant. They were actually there as a cleaner to take care of the job at hand. They were to make sure they covered it up so that it wouldn't tie any of us to it.."

Cole's eyes widened. As Richard continues to spit out this story of my life. It just filters out of him as if he has practiced this over and over till he had it perfect enough for me to believe.

They took AJ and dumped his body in a shallow grave at the bottom of a building that was in the parking lot where they met. Before it was all done, they tortured and sat him on fire for information on the money, and it all led back to Jane. His body is now a pile of ashes in a shallow grave that is now a parking garage. She has all of it, but not knowingly; I assume they passed it along with her when they gave her up. Her parents had hid one that is an heirloom to the family. I have only seen it one time. The item is priceless because it is a one of a kind, but in the right hands it is worth billions. I have tried researching it to see what it was, but no straight path to follow. I thought maybe they would help and part ways with it when we found out your mother had cancer, but they wouldn't talk about it other than they could not sell it. Something that valuable would mean it was worth more money than I have ever seen. After that conversation, things got awkward between the four of us and we quit going around them. After the funeral, they came and gave their condolences, but nothing since then.All the information is in Jessica's house, but we haven't been able to locate it. That is one reason why I needed you to get her out of the house the other day to see if the cash was there and maybe some type of documents that will lead to the artifact. To see if I could get it back without things having to get serious, but no luck in the matter of finding it. This artifact will go a long way to make the boss Mr. Demetri move along with your initiation into the organization and for me to get back into their good graces. If not, we might look over our shoulders for a while.

The room drops quiet as I sit there staring at my drink. Looking at Richard, I watch as he squirms in his seat waiting for me to lose my shit.

"So you're telling me my whole life has been a sham? That you wanted me to get close to a woman to get one over on her and then, and then have the audacity to tell me at a later date and time that she is in actuality my sister from parents that didn't even want me?" "All because some asshole gave his first child away and told his wife she had died all to cover his own ass?" "Wow what a shitty situation you are putting me into."

Just nodding my head in disbelief, I stand up and walk away to the other side of the room to give me some space. "*Are you telling me all this to make me want to care because if you are its not working, in fact, all it is doing is pissing me the fuck off."*

Pissed and wallowing in self pity as I pace the floor but only for a second because it makes me angry enough that I tell Richard "*I'm in whatever the cost, my life has been chosen for me and if she doesn't like the outcome, she only has our birth parents to blame." I need to change my future and take my life in my own hands from now on and be damned if anyone says otherwise.*

"Don't look at me to stop you. I just figured since all this was coming out, you should know what I was asking you to get yourself into."

Sitting here staring at Cole unraveling all this mess in the first place was the last thing I, as a father, wanted to do to him. But circumstances have changed and we need to adapt and overcome. I fear this is about to send him spiraling down a dark path that I won't be able to stop or control when this is all over. It will be up to him as soon as I give him the last piece of the puzzle. *"Cole, there is a job I need you to do, and it needs to be done today."*

"I need you to take Jane out for me today. I need this to be over and done."

With a dark hollow stare on Cole's face he asks *"like take out, take out? Or just to get her away for a while?"*

"Cole, I'm going to need you to get this done and without me walking you through this like an infant. Now, can you handle this or not?"

With that confused and bewildered look upon his face, I watch and see the look fade from child to man in the matter of a split second. His response to my question makes even the hair on the back of my neck stand up with chills on this wet and foggy fifty-five degree day.

"Tell me where," Cole replies, so unfeeling and detached as he could possibly be.

The address is 62nd and Kennedy St. It is Jessica White's home, your birth mother's home. Telling me the address as if I needed directions.

"Okay, quit stalling and tell me what you need done because if memory serves me correctly, I agreed I would do what you couldn't do." Cole's cold response to the message was direct and quite clear and in a way that proved me right that he has what it takes to make it in this line of business, the ability to shut it off when need be.

"*Good, because you need to get this done or we're all in deep shit. It is now a survive or die situation and I don't know about you, but being at the bottom of the food chain is not my goal.*"

"*There is a passageway in the bottom of the house that has an entrance to it from the dining room floor. All you have to do is move the rug out of the way and you will see the hatch on the floor. That is where all this needs to take place. There is a tunnel that leads to an abandoned home on the other side of the park that has everything you will need to cover your tracks. With it being dark and damp, the sound stays contained within the walls to minimize the sounds of the job. Make sure there is no evidence left that could possibly tie you or me to the murder."*

Cole grins and it makes me wonder why, but before I could ask, he spits out in anger, *"thought you weren't going to walk me through it like a child?"*

"Call when it's done. Richard barks! *I will give further instructions then."*

Cole grabs his drink on the table in front of him and throws his head back and downs it without hesitation, then slamming it down on the table and says *"No matter the cost"* gets up and walks out the room and heads to the elevator. As Cole gets in and the elevator door closes in front of him, I no longer see a child that his mother and I raised. I now see AJ written all over his face and that scares even me, knowing the path he went down.

Riding the elevator to the bottom floor, my mind races with all the thoughts of *the what ifs and the whys, but nothing changes the fact of the matter that this is my life now and that's it?*

Octavia C. Penn

"What the fuck" screaming as I punch the wall of the elevator door.

Walking to my car, I leave down the steps where the two men were promptly standing at the beginning of this meeting and I give them this nod as I walk by and it's as if they knew what it meant. *Of course, they knew what it meant thinking to myself as I picked up the pace. They work for the mob. That nod is universal for all wise guys.*

Don't ask me what I was thinking, because right now I need to be cold and unfeeling. *I know what needs to get done, but not sure how this is going to play out. How do I look Jane in the face and not feel for my friend? Hell, my sister. What I am about to do is a big ask for anyone, much less someone associated with the mob.* The long drive over to the house gives me enough time to play all this out in my head. I am going to park the car just like last time so that I could watch for when Jane enters the home. Then I will go in through the opposite entrance from the abandoned home so that I can catch her by surprise and she will be none the wiser. She won't be expecting me, so this will be quick. I don't think anyone would ever put two and two together that Jane was my biological sister and that I would be the one responsible for her murder. Hell, she is supposed to be my best friend. I know I shouldn't be this angry at her because she is an Innocent as I am in the matter, but if it wasn't for her at all none of this would have happened.

About fifteen minutes go by and I pull up to the house where I can have a clear view of Jessica's Brownstone but also where I can't be made out and put the car in park. Now I need to get myself in the right headspace for this because I know no matter how fast this goes, she is still going to struggle and it will be next to impossible to turn off my emotions.

The house that Richard described to me is just that, an abandoned house that has no business being in this neighborhood. It's just a blank canvas of brink and windows with an overly sized wood and iron door. Resembles an old world prison that you would read in an old novel. Almost turn of the century. Making my way around back to the basement entrance, and looking for the hidden key under the stone planter on the step of the porch. I quickly try to unlock the basement door so I am not seen. I hear a car slow down in front of the house. Pausing for a quick second; I see Richard make his way around the corner as I am ducking behind the stairs.

"What are you doing here?" Cole asks angrily

"I wanted to just make sure one last time you could go through with this and not back out." Richard stops with a blank stare on his face, waiting to hear a response other than the one he needed to hear.

"I told you no matter what, I am taking my life back, and no one is going to stop me."

"Okay, that's what I needed to hear. I will let you get down to it, then. Remember to call when the assignment is complete and I will relay the next steps for you. Don't forget Cole!"

"I know! Now get lost, so I can do this!"

BRYCE

Stepping out of the elevator, Blake makes a beeline straight to her desk that is right outside of my office and plops down in her chair. She automatically places her earphones in her ear. Just like that, she disappears into her own little world. Blake has been my assistant for the past three years. I believe she came straight here the day she graduated high school.

Walking past her she says that "*all the necessities for the day are on my desk and don't dare thank that I am going to drive anywhere.*" Then back into her own little world, she goes.

Shutting the door behind me, I stop and stare at the quiet of the day awaiting me. Still not hearing from Jane, so I am going to give her till lunch and then I will go looking for her. Sitting down, I now realize that missing two days of work was like the world ended. The umpteenth million missed emails and all the missed phone calls that have deadlines to call them back, two missed calls from the mayor about the murders that seemed to be connected and she wants some answers. I've got my day made for me.

Blake comes on the phone intercom to tell me, *"she received a text message from Jane but it is just a location drop pin."* Unlike last time when I showed up, she was nowhere to be found. At least she had the sense to send her location even when she won't pick up my phone call. So with that taken care of, I just send her a short message of *when she is done with work. I will have someone drop me off at her home. Not to worry about coming back to the office, so we don't miss each other.*

Staring at the computer screen long enough to lose track of time and realizing that it is almost time to call it a day. Even though I have only been here since about noon. I call Blake into the office and she comes in like she was on a mission as I tell her *"to call me a ride share. I will need it to take me to my place, then to Janes."* She nods with that childish smirk on her face and leaves the office with little pep in her step.

"Shut the door!" I holler and with no response from her to close the door, I take it as it is and just move on with closing out this long and boring day of mine.

My phone vibrates as I get a text on it and I grab it before it vibrates itself on to the floor. It is just the ride share, letting me know they are out front waiting for me. Grabbing my briefcase and personals, I head out the door for the day.

Kind of nervous on the ride to the apartment that's not even two blocks from the office. We make it there in one piece, giving me the ease to breathe, so I thank the man and get out. Getting upstairs, I shut the door behind me and beeline to the shower real fast; I change my clothes and bandages before I head out to see Jane. Stepping out of the shower, I reach for the towel to dry off and my phone vibrates once again. Once dried off, I saw that my rideshare left but offered another driver as they would be there waiting downstairs when I was ready.

Suddenly an aggressive knock on my door rattles me, thinking who in their right mind knocks like that? I automatically assumed it was my driver and boy, was I wrong. As I opened the door I was in for a rude awakening and my attitude shifted from curious to nervous instantly.

A man with a ski mask on is holding a gun level at my head and backs me back into my apartment, closing the door behind him. With him holding the gun on me, he tilts his head toward the door and tells me to lock it. Knowing damn well that when I do, all hell is going to break loose and I won't have any control over the situation. Slowly reaching for the door to lock it, the man tells me "*to turn around slowly and to keep my hands visible or we will have more than one problem.*"

"What do you want?" I ask, trying to gain some information for my advantage.

He just groans to *"Shut up! You will find out shortly what I am doing here when the time is right!"*

Wondering if this has something to do with Jane and if so, is this why I can't get a hold of her? I shout at him impatiently, *"Where is Jane and what have you done to her?"* He the walks over to me and hits me with the butt of the pistol that he is carrying and tells me to *"Shut the fuck up for the last time!"*

All the injuries that I have gained in the past few days, being hit in the head again, was not what I needed to have done to me. *So shutting up for the time being was probably my best bet for me and Jane, if they do have her?* Watching all of his movement and trying to make as many mental notes of his behavior as I could so I could identify him when all this was over was the second thing on my mind.

I watched him pace back and forth, watching his phone like whatever he was waiting for was taking too long to come to fruition. Realizing he was growing impatient, I asked him, *"Now can I ask why you are here without you smashing a pistol against my face?"*

He walks behind me and shoves me into the direction of the kitchen and points at the chair and tells me to "*take a seat and place my arms behind me."* Not wanting this to end badly, I just do what he wants me to do, no fuss. Thinking that *this motive sounds familiar.* He whips out some zip ties and begins strapping them to the bars of the chair. Not leaving any room whatsoever for me to wiggle free or to defend myself if need be.

The phone rings in the distance where the man in the ski mask was sitting. The sudden sound of the ringing made me flinch about as fast as he reached down to answer it. Whatever it was, he wasn't happy with the news that was relayed to him. He hangs up and walks around the corner out of sight where I couldn't see what he is doing and next thing that I know; I hear the door click shut, and it goes completely quiet. Not sure where to start to work myself free, I looked around, wishing I wasn't such a clean freak. Trying to get my chair to scoot across the floor to my kitchen counter, not really knowing how I am going to get the knife out of the draw when or if I do make it.

Pausing for a quick second as I hear some voices come from the other side of the door. They are approaching rapidly this time, but not so quietly, unlike when he surprised me at my door the first time.

Bang!

The door slams open, hitting the wall this time and more than just one man comes barreling into the kitchen toting tape, rope, and a black hood. This is alarming more than you could ever imagine. At this point, they are going to have to do all the work. I'm not going to make any part of this easy on them.

"What did you do to Jane?"

"I said shut up!" the man that seems to be the lead of the pack also leans in and lands a punch right in the mouth tasting my blood. Followed by the three men handling me out of the chair. They aggressively force a piece of tape over my mouth, attached mostly to the swollen lip and blood. Cutting the zip ties free but automatically replaced with rope, bounding my hands once again but in front of me.

The original man in the ski mask forces a black hood over my head and says, *"Don't make any moves or cause any ruckus to draw attention to us or you will regret. Not just for you, but for whoever tries to help. I suggest you do as you are told." I wonder what happened to the original driver that was supposed to take me up to Janes. Hoping nothing happened to an innocent person because of all of this.* Waiting for the elevator door to slide open to get in, I hear someone holler from down the hall to *"please hold the door"* as they try to catch up and all I hear is a gun go off in the distance. Squirming as I hear the ringing of the shot that was just fired off in this narrow hall. Not a second later, the man, the culprit, the murder… rounds the corner as he shoves his pistol in his belt. Like he didn't just eliminate an innocent human being. All I want to do is ask if the person is okay, but with the lack of control of my body, that doesn't seem to be the priority for me. Shoving me forward as the elevator doors open, we now make a sprint for a squeaking car that is coming in hot towards us. Not sure what to expect but whatever it is I don't have a chance to change the outcome of my current circumstances, so whatever they do, I hope it leads me to Jane.

Driving through town, trying to count the turns and listen to the surroundings of the city that we are passing by, we come to a screeching halt. I can hear the window roll down and I hear the man say we got the chief in the back. You can have him now. The boss said "to keep him alive till you get the call from Richard" and right there he gave it all away!

I knew I didn't like that family, not from the very beginning. They always had an agenda and hung around with some shady people. I never could prove they were doing anything, but now I have all the proof in the world to send Richards away along with his goons.

Octavia C. Penn

The man knew he messed up and decided that now I know too much, so he decided that I was to be placed on the upper floor of the warehouse of the club to keep quiet and out of the way. Opening the door on the vehicle, they yell and tell me to move it, but like last time, they are going to do all the work if they need to get me somewhere to torture or kill me.

Grabbing me by the waist, they threw me over someone's gigantic shoulder and just tote me up a small flight of stairs like I was already dead. All the while telling someone they have a delivery for the boss. They proceed to what seems to be an elevator and they shout *"to the top and don't stop."* We make it to the top and the goons place me back into a chair and tie me to it. They take a second and they rip the black hood off of my head. Looking around at my surroundings, all I can really see is an empty floor, the whole room is an entire empty floor of a building surrounded by glass windows. The only objects in the room are the chair that I am currently occupying and a table with what looks like shit that hurts.

They leave the tap on my mouth this whole time, guessing they don't want to hear my shit anymore than I would want to hear theirs. Waiting for what's coming, *I wonder if Jane is in this same situation, just on a different floor?*

A knock on the door echoes in this empty room and the man at the door turns to slide it open.

"Now what?"

JANE

I grab Cole by the leg and turn to pull him toward Jessica's dining room and Cole decides he is going to mule kick me with his other foot. Making me drop his leg and stumble around, trying to keep my balance. *I swear I have been hit and beaten more this week than I have ever been in my entire life, and I am beyond done with it.* Grabbing my handcuffs, I walk over to Cole as he is trying to get up and slap one cuff on his arm, but he then elbows me in the gut to make a getaway as fast as he could. He makes it to his feet as I buckle over, giving him the perfect moment when he grabs my pistol from me. Making a run for the dark end of the abyss that leads to who knows where.

To think about it, where did Cole come from? There is no way that he came from Jessicas especially since he was coming from the opposite direction when he appeared. It's almost like he knew exactly when and where to be.

Hollering for Cole to ***"stop"*** literally, as he is running, really made me think. *There are only a handful of people that know I am even here.*

Bryce, Blake, Cole, but he is here now? Bryce can't stand Cole, and I don't think Blake even knows he exists. This has to have everything to do with Richard, but why now?

Slowly getting to my feet as I catch my breath, I make my way down the tunnel toward where Cole disappeared into, with my gun, of all things. Using my phone as a flashlight, I look for the lanterns to light them to take away the advantage of the dark. Lighting the wick of one seemed to light them all one at a time, almost like a magic trick, when I turned the gas knob on high. The flicker of the flames gives off shadows that dance on every square inch of the space that the light touches. It's almost like something out of a scary movie where the dumb person runs in the wrong direction into harm's way instead of away from it. Like I'm about to do.

I walk for what seems like five minutes and I come to the room that I was in when I came back through time after living out Jessica's last hours. Looking around on the floor, I check to see if there is any sign of blood that would be left as a clue from when I shot Cole. *What do you know, a Bloody handprint on the handle of the doorknob?* When I hear a bit of a moan coming from behind the door. Pushing the door all the way open, I catch a glimpse of Cole sitting on the floor in front of the Bed where I was drugged. *Perfect, now all I need to do is get him handcuffed to the bed and my pistol out of the equation and I have the upper hand.*

He looks up at me when he discovers I found him and with an empty, deadly look like when you corner an animal and they have no other option but to resort to any and all violence to protect themselves.

"Cole, we need to talk and for you to tell me exactly what is going on and when you do, I will call for help, but not till then."

About twenty minutes go by and I slide down the wall opposite to Cole on the floor. I am in complete shock to find out that the man that I have been friends with for the last eight years as we shared our triumphs as well as our losses. Then he just tried to kill me all in the same day? The kicker is that he was taking orders from Richard.

"So have you been in the mob with Richard this whole time or was this a one time deal??"

Cole, taking a deep breath trying to keep himself from showing any more pain than was necessary, he mumbles. *"I have been wanting to prove myself to the mob boss for some time but have never been given the chance and when this opportunity presented itself, I took it."*

Staring at Cole directly in his face and with the most direct voice, I couldn't help but ask, *"Was being part of the organization worth my life, your Friend, for fuck's sake's your sister? We could have been more to each other. You knew I didn't have anyone in my life family wise. All you had to do was tell me and we could have figured this shit out!"*

"Is there anything else I need to know before I call the EMT's?"

Cole Perks up and says *"Richard is going to come after you for something that our parents passed down to you. It is some type of artifact in a trunk of some sort that has a large cash sum with it. The artifact is supposed to be a one of a kind and worth billions or some shit like that. The mob boss*

Demetri wants it for retribution for AJ stealing from them when he was alive. This man is dangerous, so please watch your back."

"Oh, and Jane, I am sorry!" Cole slumps over and Goes still

"Cole, Cole! Hang on, I will get you some help!"

Grabbing my phone out of my pocket and realizing it is dead, I need to get Cole some help. Screaming at him in hopes that he can hear me somehow that *"I will be back with help and to hold on."*

Leaving him lying on the floor was as traumatizing as the day was. Running to get back to Jessica's home so that I could make it to my car and get my work phone to call for help.

Finally, I can see the light from the dining room as I approach the stairs, climbing as fast as I can. I miss a step and eat it on the way back down. Getting up and not bothering to dust off, I begin the climb again. Making it to the top of the entrance and climbing out of the floor, I dart past the front door and down the stoop to the car. Reaching for the keys in my pocket, I hit unlock as I approach the passenger side to get my work phone out of the glove box. So dumb I have to wait for it to power up. Dialing my friend Erins' number, she is an EMT, and she picks up immediately.

"Hey it's me Jane and I need your help and you can't ask any questions!" out of breath trying to make some sort of sense in my mind when she says *"Okay, where do you need me and what do I bring!"*

I helped her out of a jam with a bad family situation a few years back and we have been friends since. Even with our busy lives, we usually meet up every few weeks just to catch up.

I tell her the address and that when she gets there, she will need medical equipment to treat a gun-shot wound and please hurry. Before I get off the phone with her, I tell her, *"Under no circumstances is she to un-cuff Cole and to make sure she is aware of her surroundings."* Sending her all the information on how to find Cole in a text message so she is sure not to miss any information to get to him as fast as possible.

BRYCE

A tall and brute man with no hair and a cane to help him walk struts in like he just might own the place. With a universal nod everyone of the men walks out of the room leaving him to his own vices.

"Mr. Gamble," he grumbled as he approached

Looking in his direction he reaches over and right before he snatched the tape from my lip he barks, *"I suggest you stay quiet and only speak when spoken to or you won't like what tools I will use to get you to be quiet!"*

As he pulls the tape from my mouth, he watches in fascination as blood pours from the corner of my lip. The man chuckles just a bit and says, *"well at least you listened this time."*

"Those boys that brought you here said you gave them some trouble."

"Well, for the moment, we are going to get to know one another and come to an understanding. Nod if you agree and understand what I am saying. You are going to do as I say and you will leave here walking and not in a body back as a waste of my time."

"Are we clear?" The man slams his hand down on my shoulder as he spins my chair toward a table.

Just being able to see out of my one not so beaten eye and with a splitting headache that is accompanying the other black eye, that's when I just nod yes in his direction in a vigorous motion to make sure he understands that I also understood. Whatever is on the table he seems eager to use.

"Now it is only fair that I let you know who I am, as for I know exactly who you are, Mr. Gamble."

"My name is Demetri and I am the one and only that is hosting you in my lovely place I call home."

"And those men that brought you here they work for me, so they do as I say. You won't be able to sway them to help you, so don't try."

Giving him the stare down, focusing on his every move, I respond by repeating his name like a parrot mocking him. *"Demetri"*

"Good, now that the pleasantries are out of the way, this is what you are going to agree to do."

"What makes you think that I will do anything for you since you are the one that has me tied to a chair and had his goons beat me to a pulp?"

"Well, we have a certain someone that is extremely close to you and If you don't then I will make you watch me dismantle her one piece at a time!" Demetri pauses right over my chair and creeps in as close to my face and says *"do you get it now?"*

"How do I know you're not bluffing?" Bryce asks

"*I thought you would say that."*

Demetri paces over to the table with all the tools of mass destruction and picks up a tablet. Looking down, he touches the screen just a few times and within moments he doesn't hesitate to show me a woman with a hood over her head in a chair and she looks to be out cold with her head limp and hanging.

"What the fuck are you doing? Is that Jane?"

"I see that this will work, so with that being said, again you are going to do what I need, or she gets hurt." Nodding in an approving notion, Demetri tells me what he needs me to do.

"First, I am going to untie you to show good faith that if you do as I ask, I will let her go unharmed. I am a man of my word, so with that notion, don't push me or I will have to prove my point." Takes a knife and begins to cut me free, then backs away from the chair. *"Now here are my stipulations for you to walk out of here. You are going to get Jane to let you in her house and you are going to convince her it would be in her best interest to locate and hand over the family heirloom and the trunk of cash that AJ stole from me. You do that and we will call it even and no harm no foul."*

"What makes you think she knows where it is? I don't think she even knows that AJ was her father, much less had a fortune stashed away somewhere."

"Do you even know what the heirloom looks like, or are we supposed to guess at this point?" Demetri Turns around and chunks a small paring knife in my direction and

lands it in my shoulder. *"Don't test me, Mr. Gamble. I won't have it. Now I don't care how you get it or find it, but that is a you problem not mine." Oh, and Mr. Gamble remember "Don't make it mine."*

And just like that, he turns to walk away, sliding the door open and then shut with no other thought as to what I might do. Understanding he definitely has the upper hand right now but my main concern is to find Jane. Pulling the knife from my shoulder, it seems to be stuck a little, but more than you would think. Giving the knife one more good jerk, I bit down and grind my teeth to keep myself from bringing any unwanted attention to myself. I swear that was the worst feeling when the blade's ridges slid against the muscle and tendons of my shoulder. *I think I would choose the car accident over the knife any day when it comes to pain.* Not sure if it was because I had to psych myself out to even get it out.

Gathering myself to make it out of this place, I head towards the door that Demetri had left out of. Worried I will meet a tall burly man on the other side of it, ready to kick my ass, I open slowly and cautiously.

"No one?" Now is my chance to get out of here. With only one way to get out, I figure that is the way I came in, so in the elevator I go. The doors open and I dart out as fast as I can. Stopping half way to what I make out to be the front entrance when I noticed that there was no one in the building. Curiosity gets the better of me for a split second, causing me to look around and nope, not a single person in sight.

"Wonder where they all went?"

Running out to the road, I see a car; quickly I get in with no hesitation and what do I see is the keys are in it, ready to go? No questions asked. I buckle in and drive it like I stole it. Sliding around the gravel drive, I throw it in gear and head straight to Jane's home.

Cole and Richard

Climbing down into the basement, closing the doors behind me, I watch Richard disappear behind the doors. Everything is dark down here. Reaching for my phone to turn the light on, I look around to study my surroundings. Uttering to myself out loud, *"this place looks like it hasn't been touched since the dark ages."* Cobwebs all over the place with maybe a few inches of dust covering what is still standing in its wake.

Making my way through the house basement, I find the door to the tunnel. This door is of a heavy metal that opens upward from the floor. Standing over the gaping hole, I see the ladder that enters a dark chasm. The hole itself is jagged, like they just took a sledgehammer and smashed the concrete floor until they had an opening. Everything about this has my stomach in an unease. Richard painted a very clear picture and even if I wanted to not do this, it still puts Jane in danger, including myself. Sounds a little self-serving, but at least it is me and not a stranger. That is the only thing that I can think of to justify my actions. At least that's what I tell myself.

Carrying on into the dark chasm, I make the bottom of the ladder when my foot hits a hard but damp surface. Not realizing that I was that close to the floor, it jars me and the phone falls out of my pocket and hits the floor. Making a constant echo down the eerie tunnel that I have turned around to meet. Shaking off the uncertainty, I pick up the phone, trying to decide where it would be best to hide. All these dark shadows give me a great opportunity for a quick and speedy job.

Sliding my phone into my pocket, I felt the wall to find my way around, remembering that Richard said there was a room on this end of the tunnel with a door. Finding it in the dark is seeming to be a little more challenging, and it seems like I will never make it to the room. When finally my finger runs across the steel hinges of what you would describe as a door.

Now with certainty that I have found where this is going to take place, I back my back up against the wall and wait out the time in silence. Hopefully I will hear some sort of noise coming from Jane in the distance. Sitting down on the ground in the dark with nothing but my thoughts and emotions.

It seems like they are all over the place at this moment. The adrenaline is kicking my ass and has me exhausted. If I wasn't so determined, I would just close my eyes and rest.

Suddenly, I hear a vague noise from the distance, and I quietly climb to my feet. The sound is almost like someone is crying uncontrollably. I take off into the dark at a steady pace when I see a vague shadow of a person sitting on the floor. *Now is my time.* I quickly pull a mask over my head to conceal my face from Jane. *Her hair is hard to miss with the vibrance of the red falling around her face.* Getting closer to her, she hollers, ***"Stop!"*** repeatedly with fear.

Then I notice she has drawn her pistol and intends to shoot me. Before I could think of moving out of the way, she fired off a shot in my direction and she didn't miss. In fact, she hits me in the stomach about a quarter inch to the side. This felt like someone took a hot knife from the fire and sliced through me at a slow rate. Making it seem like it took its sweet time, leaving a mark on my soul on its way out.

Stopping me in my tracks, I grab the side of my stomach with both hands. I can feel the warm red liquid ooze from my body. With the pain kicking in from the round, I follow gravity the rest of the way down to the ground, with my body collapsing beneath me. It takes just a second or two and I feel Jane walk over and place her hand onto my head, getting ready to pull the mask off and reveal my identity.

"I holler for her to stop!," but it was too late. I watch her face as it goes from angry and pissed to confused, all in the same breath, not believing what she just witnessed. As I lay here on the ground with her hanging over me, about a million questions came out of her mouth. But not one of them was *"Are you okay, Cole? Or I am sorry I shot you!" There I go again with my selfish ways, never mind the fact that they*

sent me here to eliminate her. Guess I shouldn't blame her, then her quick response is, *"Cole, what the hell are you doing?"* With my angry response *"You will never understand why I am here!"* The screaming ensues with the banter. *This is enough,* I thought, jumping as fast as I can as I lunge at Jane. I miss, I miss bad. Jane is quicker than she makes out to be and she grabs me just as quickly and shoves me to the ground. I end up eating a face full of dirt and not in the slow and sly way, if you catch my drift. *That bullshit could have gone better for me if I knew what I was doing. It is as if I was sent here to fail, no training and no help in sight if anything went wrong.*

I tell Jane, *"you have had life handed to you and I have had to work for everything! Yes, your parents died, but at least you came out on the other end doing well for yourself. I tried to tell you what was going on with me and what was going to happen, but you shrugged me off!" So as far as I am concerned I am not your brother because sisters wouldn't treat their brother this way!*

Confused look upon her face, Jane questions me with *"What do you mean, sister and brother? Cole, you better start talking or so help me god you won't like how I treat you in a minute!"* Jane gets so angry with me she reaches down to grab me by my ankle and haul me up the dark tunnel towards Jessica's house, but I won't let her get the best of me. *If she is willing to shoot me or turn me in, I guess I mean nothing to her.* So with my one free foot, I kicked her as she was attempting to drag me, which in all honesty she wasn't getting anywhere fast and stumbled just enough to expose her pistol and let me go.

Taking that as an out for this moment, I jump up and grab her pistol for myself and make a run for it in the opposite direction. As I am leaving, my blood is pumping overtime to make up for the blood loss and the extra adrenaline helping me bleed out even faster. Yeah, the science of the body is fascinating and disturbing all at the same time. *Think about it, it is trying to help me but give it the chance because of my current circumstances I will bleed out so case in point, trying to kill me.* Making it back to the end of the tunnel, and realize I do not have the strength to climb that ladder to get out of here. I decide to just go inside the room with the steel door and wait out the last of my miserable living and breathing life. *Maybe she will pass up the room and think that I went up the ladder and escaped, leaving me to just die alone.* Without having to save face and make Jane feel bad for something that I had done. *If I could just tell her I am sorry and that if I could go back and do it all over again I would and change the outcome.*

Meir seconds goes by and the door slowly opens. I don't even look up at first but Jane opens the door and just stands there in the doorway dead silent, judging me. I could feel her eyes on me and I turned to look at her. For a brief second I am happy she is here but it quickly fades as I begin to cough up some blood. Jane walks over and quickly slaps the other end of the handcuffs to the bottom of the bed that I was leaning against. She then kicks the pistol away from me and I don't even fight her for it.

Jane asks me *"to please tell her everything"* and scolds me for not having enough faith in her to tell her. *Even if I didn't have enough time to deal with it, I would have listened if it was of this magnitude. Friendship and family meant everything to her and I am dumb to not believe that of her. The only thing I see fit to do is to apologize to her and hope she understands when I tell her everything that Richard has planned for her.*

Blacking out is in my near future as everything starts to have an echo effect to it and the room is splotchy fading black with every passing moment. Jane gets up off the floor from in front of me. I can hear her leave and shouting she is getting help to just hold on.

Jane

I received a text from Erin telling me she made it to the house and she would take care of the *"problem"* and wait for further instructions and also not to worry. *With a sigh of relief, it makes the drive up to my house a bit easier.* I slam on the brakes and, not even turning the engine off, I dart up the stairs into my home. Shutting the door behind me, I lock all the devices on the door, including the chain. *"Jane!"* With a slow and low voice startles me and as I turn around to see who it was, it is Bryce.

"Bryce, what happened to you? You look worse than when you were in the hospital!"

"Thanks Jane! You look amazing as well. We need to talk, and you're not going to like it."

"If it is about Cole or Richard, I am already up to speed on it, thanks, but I am handling it!"

"Wait, Jane quickly changes her course of questions. Is that what happened to you? Did they do this to you?" I'll kill'em!

The look on Bryce's face says it all. He doesn't even need to say a word and I know that it was them that did this. I run into his arms and hug him, not quite sure who is hugging harder when we both flinch in pain from our wounds. Bryce repeats, *"We need to talk."* Worried about where this is going based on how we both look and with what has happened to me in the past hour, I take a deep breath. *"Okay, Bryce, you have my attention. What is it?" "Can we at least sit down for this? " he* mummers. Walking through the entryway and into the living room, we find a place on the couch. He sits at one end as I sit at the other, not ready to hear the bad news that he is about to hit me with. *So I brace myself and yep, there it is, Richard, in every sentence that comes out of his mouth.*

"So you're telling me that Richard had the mob kidnap you out of your own home and bring you to some warehouse to beat information out of you?"

"Kinda seems like it when you put it that way. It seemed to take longer in person." As he tries to chuckle in the mists of all the pain.

"*Nice to know you still have your sense of humor intact. But I don't find this the least bit funny"* as with every word Jane raises her voice. *"They just tried to kill me! Is that what you want to hear to make this more real for you? Something is going on with me and I can't even put it into words, much less the fact that my so-called 'friend' Wait, wait, I mean Brother just tried to get rid of me."* By now I am screaming at the top of my lungs, sounding like a raving lunatic, when in all actuality I am just scared. I think I might have made it all too real for myself now. Standing in front of him, tears fall down my cheek. Not wanting him to see me cry like this, I turn away and hide my face in my hands.

That is the moment that I feel his hand placed onto my shoulder. Bryce gently spins me around and wraps his arm around me as if it was the most natural thing in the world. The smell of him, even after being battered and beaten, is still comforting. He raises his hands and slides it just under my eyes onto my cheeks to wipe the tears away.

The hesitation is losing its power and I can't take it anymore. My emotions get the better of me and I go in for the kiss. Both of his hands rising to meet my face, he pulls me up and towards his lips even more than I thought possible. His lips are so soft and seductive, making me want to nip at them in a playful manner. He pulls back with a small hiss, forgetting in the heat of the moment that he has sustained an injury to his lip. I raise my hand and place it on the edge of my lip as to feel where his lips were just touching mine. The urge to bite down on his lip fades as I bit my own; sending a small signal to him saying that I liked the kiss. Maybe more than I should have.

Bryce Quietly says with a low and bolstering growl, *"Are you sure you want this? Because I don't think I will be able to stop myself if we start?"* Hair on my skin raises and my pupils widen thinking of the kiss and what he just said to me. Thinking of what is about to take place has my body temperature rising, making the lower regions of my body pulse out of control. I give him a slow seductive nod, then turn around and head towards the bedroom, hoping he understood that I wanted him to follow.

Catching a glimpse of myself in the mirror as I pass, trying to see if he was in fact following and self doubt rears its ugly head. *It has been too long. What if he sees me and decides this 'Staring at myself' isn't worth it?*

Never really thinking that this moment would occur, much less after being beaten or assaulted. Knowing all the bruises and marks on my body makes me look less attractive, 'well at least to me I am not something to ogle over'. But Bryce is all smiles as I stand in the mirror, destroying any doubt I ever had about myself.

Bryce asks *"What are you staring at in the mirror?"* My hesitation gives off exactly how I feel and he snaps me around to tell me, *"You are beautiful."*

He reaches down and wraps his arms around my thighs just below my ass and picks me up, walking in the direction of my bedroom as if he knew where he was going. At this point, I don't care if it is in the bathroom. Well, maybe I do just a little. There are no soft surfaces and limited space to do the things that I want to do. Bryce pushes me into the door. I grab the handle to turn and we push through the threshold. He then pauses and looks around and shakes his head in approval. With a chuckle, I ask *"Why do you look so shocked about my room?"* In this moment he gave the perfect answer *"The bed is bigger than I thought it would be!"*

Dropping me to the floor slowly, he plants another kiss, but this time on my forehead. He then walks away and heads to the bathroom, confused as to what he is doing, but then I hear the shower turn on. I walked into the room where Bryce had disappeared to and saw him in the shower. Thinking *that was a fast undress.* The glass panels leave nothing to the imagination. The perfectly chiseled man that is standing in my shower with water beading off of him. Trying to look calm, but then he demands, *"Get in!" Who on earth would take this long to get in? Guess that would be me!* Beginning to take my clothes off, I start by undoing the buttons of my jeans, then my shirt goes shortly after. Standing there in a pile of my clothes with nothing left but a bra and thong, the chill makes my nipples show through the lace. I see Bryce reach down to grab his cock, but the steam of the water has fogged up the glass by now, so now I can't see him stroking it. That was all I needed to know and off the rest of the garments went. Opening the door, the steam clears the stall and reveals what I kind of already knew. Bryce was very much well endowed, plus some. *When they say aged like fine wine, they meant it.* He grabs me by the waist and pulls me under the shower water. The rain setting on the shower head feels perfect, not too hard but just right, beating against the bruises and open wounds. I lean my head back, letting the water hit me on the face and Bryce takes the opportunity to place his mouth on my neck. Wrapping his lips around me, he slides his teeth against the surface of my skin, causing a chill and for me to moan without warning. I can feel him smile. He slowly and deeply growls *"That's my good girl"* and with that one line, he took a seven to a fifteen in two seconds.

Hoping that he was the kind of man that liked to take charge and boy, was I right. He spun me around to face the wall with one hand and bent me over with the other. *Glad that we are in the shower because I think he might have already made me cum with all the commanding of my body.* Ready to feel his penis push through the opening of my vagina, he lifts my leg and places it firmly on the corner seat. I can feel Bryce's hand navigate my body as I hear him crouch down on his knee. Bryce leans in, slides his tongue between my thighs and up to the opening of my pussy, and continues to the back end of my ass. Shocked that I really liked it, I feel two fingers caress my clitoris and circling in slow motion. Making my back dip in pleasure, I force my leg back down to the shower floor. I turn to grab him by his hair and tug in an upward motion. Standing up and smiling with his grayish blue eyes he calmly whispers in my ear *"I like it, now wash off and come join me in the bed."* Bryce steps out of the shower and grabs a towel and says staring at me *"you're going to need this"* hangs it on the hook next to the shower door.

Lathering the soap onto my body as my eyes are closed, I run my hand between my legs and message myself. After the suds are all gone and I smell clean, I reach over and turn the water off and get out.

With a low faint voice, I can hear Bryce singing along with the music that he had playing on the Bluetooth speaker next to my bed. The lights are off besides the low lit lamp and some candles from the other night that I had lit while in the tub flicker in a seductive dance. I don't know if he realizes how amazing he looks until he looks up and catches me smiling.

Making my way to the bed with the conscious decision to go through with this even though he is my boss, he demands, *"Get on the bed and hold still!"* My eyes widen and I do as I am told by first placing both of my hands on the bed, then followed by my knee crawling my way to the top where the mattress meets the headboard. *"Like this,"* I replied as I turned over to lay on my back. With a shaking motion of *no*, he takes a finger and spins it around, meaning he wants me turned over. This man grabs me by my ankles and slides me closer to the bottom of the bed. He says, *"Do you need a safe word or can I do as I please?"*

With that said and how bad my body wants him, I quietly say, so he has to lean over the back of my body. *"No words needed. I'll take all of you the way you want me to!"* With him laid on top of me from behind, he puts a little pressure on my throat with one hand. Followed by him, biting me on the back. *"Now grab the railing and don't let go till I tell you to,"* he applies a bit of pressure on my pelvis by shoving his cock between my legs. Making his way down my body, he takes the same hand and cups my breast so that he is now standing in a ready position. Legs shaking with adrenaline, I am ready to feel the girth of his cock in me. He takes his hand and places a few fingers into me and moves them in a fucking motion. I can feel his eyes on me and if I could feel his eyes on me, then I know he can feel how much I want him with the way he needs no lubrication to just slip in. The tip of his cock has a piercing through the top and out of the bottom with a large piercing inserted. I can feel every inch of this man's body and everything he wants to do to me comes off of his body in an electric wave. He slaps me on the cheek, taking all hands off of me, making me work my hips in a rotation motion, feeling every inch of his cock as I control the speed in and depth.

God, how am I supposed to last? I am already weak. I can't imagine him being able to hold off?

"Turn around and get on your knees, Jane."

Doing as he says without hesitation, he grabs the back of my head with a hand full of my hair in his fist and places his cock in my mouth.

"No hands Jane!"

How this man says my name makes me quake. With the slow thrusting of his body and my head up against the end of the bed, I have nowhere to go but to swallow every inch of his penis.

"Enough," he growls! "*I hope you're ready."*

oh god ready for what?

Bryce Picks me up and places me on the edge of the bed and puts both legs over his shoulders. Slowly shoves the tip of his cock into my wet pussy, leans over and says, *"No word?"* I just nod and pull him closer by his arms and he takes that as giving it all to me. Continuing by pushing the rest of his cock into me, I arch my back and gasp. Bryce begins slowly working his way into a perfect rhythm. As I relax and enjoy the amount of girth, Bryce notices and picks up speed.

Taking both of my legs off his shoulders, he puts my legs together, twisting my lower half to one side. Using me as an anchor and slamming his body into mine, I holler, "*Daddy!*"

Bryce leans closer and places his hand over my mouth in a kinky manner, whispers "*not a word I meant it!"* He then takes his hand and places it around my neck and gives it a slight controlling squeeze. Never missing a beat.

Moaning because he is so turned on, he just knows what he wants but also how to please me in the process. He slows down and makes a low grunt, pushing me just a bit up the bed. Flipping me on my stomach once again. Bryce climbs over the top of me and straddles me with my legs together, telling me to "*tilt my hips outward.*" He slaps my ass again and forces his cock into me a bit more, demanding this time. Bryce takes his hand and places it on the headboard and one next to me for leverage and balance to keep me from sliding away as he pounds into me.

Thinking to myself, *This is my favorite position.* The moaning gets louder, and the breathing gets heavier, I holler out *"Daddy"* again and he bolsters *"Cum Jane, Cum hard!"* then smacks my ass again and he picks up speed but the thrusts get shorter and he stops just short of going over the edge and pulls out just in time as it sprays across my back. I can feel his body shaking just as violent as mine.

With me laying there for a second, he grabs the towel that he told me I would need when I was in the shower and cleans me off. As if he couldn't get enough, he kisses me on the head, murmurs in exhaustion, *"Beautiful"* before he turns and heads for the bathroom to shower once more.

"I'll be back to hold you after we clean off you coming?" Bryce asked, and it was just that the fastest wash off and back into the bed to relax as we let the world slip

away, or so I thought. Bryce whispers into my ear, *"There is a matter of Cole and Richard. We need to take care of it!"*

He can't seem to help himself and just give me this night and leave well enough alone. It ended perfectly till now!

"I know I left Cole handcuffed to a bed in a passageway under Jessica's house with an EMT!" Bryce pulled me around to face him, stunned and worried.

"What the hell, Jane! you didn't think to tell me before now?"

Bryce

God, this woman is beyond beautiful. She is also intelligent and for me to be here with her in her home is something special. Wanting to do many things to her and I now get the chance. This all is flying by so quickly and all I want to do is keep her here and keep her safe. In this moment though I get to love her.

Warning her that once we start I won't be able to help myself and in which case if she needs a safe word, now is the time to say so.

Picking Jane up to carry her to the bedroom, I take both hands full of her ass and lift her up, wrapping her legs around my waist. They fold around me like two puzzle pieces that fit together perfectly. Pushing her into the door, she anticipates what I needed and opens it. Setting her down on the ground, I turn to look at the bed, thinking, *perfect.* She smiles and I strip as I head to what I believe to be the bathroom to jump in the shower. *I don't want this perfect moment to be ruined and overshadowed by all the blood and dirt. I might be a man, but I am a gentleman and I see how Jane presents herself and keeps a nice home.*

I climb into her shower and make it as steamy as possible, scrubbing off the remnants of the evening, and Jane comes through the door. She has a smile on her face. She stands in front of the glass door and that is when I grab my penis and begin to stroke it. I tell her to *"Get in."* This woman looks me up and down, then she slowly undresses herself as I watch. Jane opens the shower door, and the steam clears just enough to show the figure of her supple body. I take her into my arms and she closes her eyes and tilts her head back into the water. I can't help but stare at her neck and breast. I steal a kiss as I can't hold off any longer, so I spin her around and place her foot on the shower seat. *"I will taste her before she tastes me!"* Thinking to myself as I drop down to slide my tongue into her pussy to get a taste of her hot wet body. My cock is growing and stiffening faster than I want her to know as I am stroking it. I stand up to wipe away Jane's sweet nectar from my mouth.

Jane turns around, not being able to keep from going over the edge, and I tell her in a low growl, *"to wash off and join me in the bed!"*

Getting a towel and drying off, I set the mood. I strut into the room, hoping that she is getting an eye full. I reach to turn the lights off so that when I flick her lamp on for a low ambiance feel and light some candles along with some music. Catching me off guard, I turned to see Jane smiling at me while I was singing and dancing in the nude.

With her hair wet and the glow of her skin against the light from the bathroom, she looks like she had just stepped out of heaven. I don't think she even knows how beautiful she is, but tonight I am going to show her how much I think she is. I am going to touch every inch of her body by the time this night is over.

The night goes amazing and laying in this big bed of hers, the silence creeps in and the obvious topics seem to take over. *"Jane, we need to talk about Cole and Richard."* Just like that, I turn her around and with her eyes widened she tells me, she left Cole with a gun-shot wound handcuffed to a bed with her friend Erin, the EMT.

"What? Why didn't you tell me this sooner?"

With a spit of anger, the words just fell out about how Richard's boss Demetri has threatened my life and whoever he has captive in a room. *We need to go to Cole and find out what he knows so that we can figure out a plan before anyone else has to die.*

I sling the covers off and get dressed. *"Where are you going at this time of night?"* Jane asks in a concerned tone.

"We don't have time to waste and I am going to Cole and if he doesn't talk, then I will find Richard and make him talk!"

"It is time this all comes to an end! I'm going to go by the house then I will meet you at Jessicas. Let's just hope and pray that Cole can tell us more." Stopping real quick in the door frame, I turn to Jane and make the odd comment, *"I can't believe Cole is your full biological brother,"* then I turn to leave the room.*I know leaving her with that last sentence was harsh, but it just fell out of my mouth. But for real, Jane fell far from that family tree.*

Scurrying to the front door, noticing it is open, stopping in my tracks, someone grabs me around the mouth. *"Don't make a sound. Now move, we're going to take a ride."* The same hooded people standing in the street at the base of the stairs. So I am guessing Demetri sent them. This time they take me back to the warehouse, but no hood or hands are bound. *Guess they knew I was going to do anything to keep Jane safe, even if I wasn't.* We pull up, but this time no guards are standing out front. Everyone gets out of the car but me and Mr. Demetri. *"Now, since you seem to have had your fun for the evening, I thought I would remind you of what you are supposed to be accomplishing. So when the doors open, I would hope that you do not make a run for it or Richard will have to shoot you."*

"I am listening and I assure you I won't run. But Jane wasn't the person in the chair, so who is it?" Bryce orders.

"That is exactly what I am going to show you. I am going to give you a little bit of motivation to get what I need done, so follow me."

The car door opens, and he exits like it's just business as usual and heads for the door of the warehouse. I follow as the curiosity is overwhelming. *Who could he have in the chair? Everyone I know is gone out of state.*

Following Demetri up the stairs, an eerie feeling comes over me. Instead of going up the elevator, we went down a set of stairs that I seemed to miss the first time I was in this place. It is just like you would imagine a mob kingpin would have, a dungeon of some sorts in his basement. Reaching the bottom of the stairs, we come to a short hallway ending into a door to a room. Demetri turns and says, *"You can go in but she can't come out, not till our business is concluded. Do you understand?"* Nodding in agreement, he unlocks the door and Richard moves to the side of the door from behind me to keep guard.

"I'll be upstairs when you're ready to talk. Richard, watch him and make sure he keeps to his word or kills him, then her."

Eyes wide, I stare at Demetri as he leaves to go upstairs and Richard opens the door. I step in and the door closes behind me. The person in the chair is making a sobbing noise, trying to wiggle her hands free. Not sure who to expect coming into this dark room with only a chain link light hanging from the ceiling just above the chair. That is it, a chair with a person strapped in and a light dangling from above.

I walk over and take the hood off of the woman that is crying and with complete shock I fall to my knees, grabbing the tape on her mouth to pull it off. She sees me and cries even harder.

It's Kelsey! What is going on? Scratch that. How do they have her and when did they snatch her?

Okay, Bryce, one calm question at a time. She is already scared and panicking.

"Bryce! you have to help me!" she quietly screams as if someone is listening in. *"Some random man in a mask grabbed me as I was leaving the hospital and threw me in a black car. They Brought me here and said I would be okay unless some job went wrong."*

"Do you have any idea what they are talking about?" With a helpless look on my face and hers, I tell her everything. I begin to tear up as I tell her that I have to leave her here to help someone, but they said they wouldn't hurt you if I got it done. Explaining that *"many people will die if I don't keep this deal. I won't be able to live with myself if they hurt any of you because of me."*

Octavia C. Penn

It looks like Demetri kept his promise; she seems to be okay other than being frightened to death. *"I will keep my promise and keep you safe, but I will have to leave you here."* She struggles with the concept and pleads with me to take her with me.

"Kelsey, they will kill both of us before I can get you out of this room. Stay here and I will come back for you, I promise!" I turn to leave and Kelsey says, *"I love you,"* just giving her a nod. I knock on the door then leave her sitting in that chair, frightened.

The door opens with Richard on the other end of it. His smug grin says it all, that he is enjoying all of the power that he thinks he holds. Throwing my hand around his throat, I shove him into the wall and tell him, *"You hurt her and I will kill you"*. With a deadly glare he says *"No problem but I get my orders from Mr. Demetri not you."* I throw a punch at Richard's stomach and as soon as he buckles over, his face meets my knee. Richard falls back onto the floor and says, *"Feel better? Make you feel like a man?"*

Walking away before I do more than beat his ass, I climb the stairs to find Demetri so that we can discuss what it is exactly that I am looking for.

Coming out of the stairwell, I walk into an open room with a bar and lots of tables and places to sit. In one corner, there is a small couch next to a window with a light and that's where I find Demetri sitting. He doesn't even look up and ask me to "*have a seat.*" Sitting down across from him, he hands me a photo of this ring. It is godly, looking almost like it shouldn't be here. Something out of fiction and that's when Demetri says, *"This is what you need to find for me. There should also be a trunk of money that AJ stole from us when he made the deal to trade children on the black market for money. I don't know about you, but I am a man that knows children are off limits and that is why he is no longer breathing on this earth. I have two daughters of my own and I'll be damned if someone ever thought about doing that to me or mine. So I am going to give you twenty-four hours to find it, then I will make sure Richard finds the motivation for your sister. Are we clear?"*

"And Just so we are clear, threats are useless to me because if you touch one hair on my sister I will make sure I burn your world down with you standing right smack in the middle of it." I narrowed my eyes in on Demetri as to show him I was not making light of this situation.

Demetri smiles and says, *"Well, at least we know where we both stand."* With that said, he waves his hand at me like he dismissed a goon to do his bidding. Standing and cautiously walking away In hopes my threat doesn't sway him to just kill me now, I speed up the escape for the door.

There is a car waiting for me at the bottom of the steps to take me to my apartment. It feels weird to just get in and not be fearing for my life to an extreme at that very moment. I understood I have twenty-four hours to get Demetri his cash and ring.

Jane

Headed to the closet to grab a pair of jeans and a T-shirt to wear, I slid one foot in the hole after the other, almost falling over, losing my balance. Doing the shimmy to pull the skinny jeans up then tossing the white T-shirt over my head, I reach down to grab my trusty combat boots. While lacing them up, this red wavy mop of hair is in my face, convincing me that I need to comb this mob on my head, as it is all in my face. Finding a ponytail in the drawer of my nightstand, I don't actually brush it. I just throw my head over, bending at the waist and pulling it up into a bun on top of my head to get it out of the way.

"There now to catch up with Bryce."

I almost forgot to grab my red leather jacket that was hanging on the foot of the bed, making sure I threw it on before entering the frigid night air.

Heading down the hall, turning the corner of the living area, I make it to the front door.

"It's open! Why would Bryce forget to leave the door open? I know he was furious when he left, but I guess he wasn't aware he did it." Turning to make sure the door is locked this time, I dash to the car and get in.

With the night air so cold and crisp, even with the speedy dash to the car in the short time I was in the open, it cut through me like a knife.

While driving, I think of what I am going to ask Cole. Lord knows I don't even know where to start. What did he expect to gain out of all of this? Thinking with a smart ass sister attitude voice in my head "*Even if he didn't get caught?"* I Hope that I could convince him that if he decides to help me get Richard, and this Demetri then it would make me forgive him a little easier or at least tip the scales more in his favor.

None of this is going to matter if Bryce kills him before I can get there and save him from being beaten to death or tortured by Erin.

Creeping up to the house, I put the car in park and turned my headlights off. It is just now sinking in. *This is where my mother lived! This is where she spent her whole life after they sold me behind closed doors! Where some sperm donor thought it was okay to take his only child at the time and sell her off to save his own ass. What a class A-jerk and piece of shit AJ would have been as a father.* To think he stayed with her and lied to her for years, much less Jessica letting him get her pregnant a second time. Maybe the best thing was that neither one of us was in that house growing up. We might have not made it. Tears begin to well up in my eyes. This is the home of the woman that was tortured and shot in the back of the head for some family artifact and a large sum of cash. "*I swear if I would have known AJ back then I probably would have killed him myself!*" Screaming at the top of my lungs in my own car getting it out of my system before I have to bottle it all back up.

Slamming my hands down on the steering wheel repeatedly because I could have known someone that actually was looking for me. Looking at the building that has my friend and now my brother that I shot in the stomach and handcuffed to a dungeon bed, wondering *if maybe I should just run away. I am already tired of all the shit that I have been through the past few days. I don't think not one person could take this torture and keep going like it was nothing, much less be running from the mob.*

Which reminds me that Demetri has told Bryce he has already gone after an innocent that is tied up in a basement somewhere just waiting for us to fail, to take her out. Turning the ignition off in the car, I notice Bryce coming from around the side street. I hurry to meet him, but he seems to be on a mission and beats me to the door. Maybe I should have hollered, but not too sure he would have even noticed. Which makes it even more imperative that I get in there before he beats Cole to death for the information. *I know Erin won't do anything to stop him if she found out his motives were in line with the mob.*

Walking into Jessica's home now that I know she was my mother makes the hairs stand on end and my mind wonders. *Why would Demetri send that man to kill her in the first place? All of this is AJ and Richard's doings. They should have paid the ultimate price, not us. Sure, it was all on Richard to cover his tracks so Demetri wouldn't get involved.* When I remember that just before he killed her, Jane saw a glimmer of the key behind a random painting in the dining room. Racing to find the object in the dining room before I head down to the tunnels to play referee, I run into a man in a ski mask. This man looks just like the one when I jumped time, but when I call him out on his sketchiness, he darts out the other direction and heads to the back door. Hollering out to "***stop***" like that ever works, I pull my pistol out aim and shoot him in the leg, *"This time I am ready."*

I don't even hesitate. I jump on top of him and handcuff him. This time taking control of the situation, making it where he can't hit me. *Now time to take the mask off, I pause for the moment. I have never met this man in my life.*

My first question for him is "Why is he here?"

He doesn't even hesitate to tell me a name *"Demetri!"*

Should have known this has him written all over it. Yanking the mask off in a violent motion, I see that *this is just a boy! No way he could have done those things to me or the others.*

This is just a kid. He couldn't be more than nineteen, maybe even twenty, if I pushed it. I lean in and ask, *"Is he here now?"* shaking his head no, he replies, *"He sent me here to check on Cole. He has been trying to get a hold of him all day and he won't answer. He sent me to collect him and to clean up any mess that he has made."*

"*Well, I am going to leave you here and you're not going to leave,"* as I place another set of cuffs around his ankle and clip it to the banister of the back hall staircase. "*I will send someone to help you as soon as I can."*

With a scared look on his face he asks *"am I going to die?"*

"Not if you do what I say now. Where is your phone?" Reaching into his pants pocket, I eventually find a phone that resembles a burner phone. Looking through it, I find nothing but one number. *"Let me guess the number is to get a hold of Demetri?"* Shaking his head in an up and down motion.

"I'll be holding on to this."

Turn to disappear, it resonates with me to get the object that was behind the frame. Sliding my hand behind it, I pull it away from the back and the whole thing comes off the wall. I pick up the photo frame and see a sonogram taped to the back where I pulled what looks to be a key. *Staring down at the photo and key, my mind wanders to where the key may go and wondering which child is this an image of?*

Enough wasting time, Jane.

Wandering into the floor of the dining room, I make my way down into the tunnel with a photo, key and a burner phone in tow. The lanterns are already lit with flames dancing down the walls in a dotted line, making it seem shorter in length. Making my way down the hall, I can see the door where I left Cole and Erin to wait out the night. Hoping when I walk into the room, I leave with the answers that I am looking for and not more mystery to unravel.

Peering into a crowded torturous dungeon with three people turning to face me, the room goes silent.

Bryce barks orders almost immediately, *"Cool it, hot pants! One, I just got here and two, I need to be caught up to speed."*

Looking at Erin, I ask her if Cole will recover and she just gives me the thumbs up and makes the quick comment, *"You could have aimed better and not needed me in the first place!"*

Snarky, but glad she helped. When she did, I just ignored the banter.

"I need you to leave me alone with Cole so I can talk to him, sister to brother." Cole throws his head in my direction in shock that I said it with remorse and not anger. Bryce just gave me a stare down. Then, when I thought he was just going to let me do this my way, he opened his mouth. I move in his direction to shove him out the door, and he and Erin force me to follow.

Going round after round with them at this point gets nobody any answers, so I just ask them to give me some time and they agree, but they were going to head back to the top. Watching Erin and Bryce disappear further into the tunnel as the lanterns cast shadows that play with your mind. I pause to gather my thoughts one more time. *Be firm, but don't make him shut down or I will get nothing out of him.*

The tunnel shakes and a loud ringing fills the tunnel like Quasimodo is ringing the tower bell after beating Frollo.

This is something new that I haven't experienced since my encounter with this whole ordeal. Now the tunnel has chunks of rock falling from the ceiling and I am trying to dart the debris as the lanterns seem to have taken a hit and went out. Scared shitless and not knowing if the next step will land a solid chunk of rock on me, pinning me down here or killing me. The next thing I know I fall, landing myself in between a literal rock and a hard place. Hoping that saves me from being squished, I curl up into a ball covering my head, trying to keep myself from dying.

The shaking stops and the sound disappears just as fast as it came on, pausing in the fetal position for just a second longer to catch my breath and that familiar smell is back.

"God, I don't have the energy to do this again!" I scream at the top of my lungs, which I know from experience does me no good. *"No! No! No!"* With the anger rising, I feel a burning in my body and a numb tingling takes over. The lights begin to flicker and I begin to fade out.

This time, when the present goes dark, I don't feel like I actually traveled anywhere. Opening my eyes, it is still dark and disheveled, but this time I am shut in the room where

Cole was. I stay quiet this time so as not to alert anyone. Learning from my past mistakes, I just try to listen to see if I can hear any movement besides my own. I hear a subtle moan like someone is hurt, and it frightens me.

"Hello?"

The person coughs. *"I know exactly how they feel."*

"Bryce?"

I hear the person shuffle and then they holler, *"Jane!"*

Shocked at the voice I hear. *It is Cole.*

Cole and Richard

I wake to a woman with brown flowing locks of hair pinned atop her head with glasses pushed all the way up the bridge of her nose. *"Kind of like what you would picture a librarian would look like."* She crouched down next to me on the floor. I guess with all the movement, I alerted her I was awake. Reacting to the sharp stabbing pain in my arm when I moved it to adjust my body, I quickly came to the conclusion that there is a needle stuck in the bend of my arm that is attached to a bag of fluids. She hollers, *"Keep still and to watch out for the IV in my arm! The next time I won't be so gentle"* then she stuck her hand in the place that radiated heat and pain immensely. I whined about it out loud and all I got was *"You wouldn't be in this position if you wouldn't have done anything stupid that involved my friend Jane."*

"Boy, did she find a feisty person to wrangle me in her absence!"

"Well, since we are getting the pleasantries out of the way, what is your name since you seem to know mine and Janes?"

"Well, you're bound to find out when she gets back, so I see nothing wrong with telling you my name."

"It's Erin. I am keeping you alive, so I suggest you be nice or I know ways to torture you until she gets here to save you from me."

"I believe she isn't lying," so with that threat, I just stay quiet. Next thing that I know, I hear Erins' phone go off with a text message. Hoping it was Jane with some news about the Demetri problem.

Waiting for her to tell me something, she places the phone back into her pocket and says nothing. *Not that my life depended on it?* I thought sarcastically.

Trying to start a conversation with a woman that, at this current moment in time, hates your guts is almost impossible. It seems like a few hours pass and the phone goes off once again, but this time Erin looks up at me and says,

"Jane is on her way."

Erin asks *"How do you feel because you have some questions to clear up?"*

The phone alerts again. She then reads out loud, *"Bryce should also be there any minute he left before I did, just a heads up, so don't shoot him."*

"Wondering why she sent Bryce?" Considering how he feels about me, this is a bad sign. If he beats Jane here, Bryce will kill me before she ever shows up, and Erin will help him. Bryce has liked me about as much as I have ever liked him. I think the only reason we haven't really clashed is for Jane's sake.

About that time, Jane's voice carries down the hall when she hollers for Erin. *"At least I know she is here and not dead."*

Demetri must not have all the information yet.

"Where is Richard?"

"I missed the deadline to meet him and he hasn't even bothered to call me."

With my one free arm, I reach into my jacket pocket and notice the phone is missing. *"Missing something?"* Erin projected as she pulled the phone out of her bag. *"Didn't need you calling your daddy to bail you out of this so, I took it and went through it while you were asleep and I've got to say you are in some deep shit."*

"Oh, and I took a screenshot of the messages and saved them, so don't try to deny anything."

Jane peers into the room and doesn't even look at me. She waves over to Erin and asks her "*to follow her and bring everything but Cole."* Jane finally stares at me and gives me the most disappointing look I may have ever seen. *"I will be back and you will tell me everything!"* Jane disappears once again into the dark hallway, making me wonder what else could I tell her when she returns. *I only know what Richard told me, and I told her all of it the last time we spoke.*

What else does she want?

The door creaked open expecting Jane to show but it wasn't. Standing there with a gun in their hand and a pissed look upon their face I fear for my life. This person has only been around when shit hits the fan and a job has gone sideways

"Where is Jane, and what did you do with her?" Confused as to who I was talking about, he replies,

"Who?"

When suddenly the room begins to vibrate and go dark. The sounds of a body hitting every surface trying to stay upright but quickly comes to an impossible feat when a thud echoes and a gun slides across the floor. Quickly hurrying with my one free hand, I blindly grab the gun to arm myself from this mobster.

The room was dark and suddenly going still. A little bit of fear arises when the thought of Jane and the other two in the hall. I hope that they are okay because the inside of this room is destroyed with the feel of rubble all around me. Great, I will never get out of this predicament if I can't get these handcuffs off of me. Twisting around and trying to feel for something that could pry the cuffs apart, I realize the leg of the bed is bent from the impact of some of the stone hitting the frame on its way down. Sliding my hands down the rail, I can barely fit the chain under the metal to get free. *"There, now I can get out of here!"*

Octavia C. Penn

Not being able to see, I stump my foot on the body of the man that just threatened me prior to the passageway taking a toll on him. The man doesn't move a bit, and I am relieved and stressed that they might be dead! *Does that make me an even worse person wanting him to be the later after I just tried to kill Jane earlier today?*

Reaching the door that was open but now is slammed shut, I try to push it as hard as my body would allow. With handcuffs on and a wound that is still fresh, it is almost impossible. I grab my side and I can feel the shirt that I am wearing becoming wet again with blood from my wound tearing open, trying to force the door to budge. Ripping the IV out of my arm to give me a bit more of an advantage to use my body to help lift and push at the same time.

The ground shakes this time harder than before and down I go. *Fine I will stay here for the time being but only long enough to gain some strength.* I lean my head against the wall and close my eyes to rest when suddenly I smell a horrible smell that takes over the room. It is almost unbearable and I choke, trying to catch my breath. I scream for help and it does no good. Panic sets in and I can't keep myself awake. I feel myself get heavy and slide towards the floor. The sounds of the room become distant and my breathing fades and I am no longer here. I wake to the darkness once again, but this time it is different. I moan a little as my wound is still sore from Jane shooting me. Reaching down to feel it, I need to perch myself up against something to take the strain off of the muscle so I can breathe without wanting to cry out.

"Maybe I should just stay laying on the floor. It seems to be the only place I can be at the moment that won't cause duress."

It takes just a second for me to throw myself down and I hear a *"Hello?"* shocked and startled from the woman's voice. I cough.

"Bryce?"

Thinking to myself, *"That is Jane, but how did she get in here?"*

"Jane?" There is a pause in the darkness of the room making it seem much bigger than it should be.

"Cole?"

BRYCE

The car Driving me to Jessica's house to meet Jane and her ridiculous new found brother is taking its sweet ass time when we come to a halt at a red light. Two more blocks is all it is going to take and we can figure out how to get my sister out of Demetris hands. This point in time the only thing on my mind is hoping that Jane has already figured out where the artifacts are and hope that the money is with it.

Finally we arrive at the house and the driver drops me off a block behind the house and says that I can walk from here. being a little annoyed I wanted to blurt out that he was a piece of shit and to go to hell. but who knows what he would tell his boss and in return they would do to Kelcey. So being the level headed person that I am I just save face and get out.

"It will give me time to gather my thoughts before I make it to the house and rip Cole a new one like I did his "dad" in the warehouse." Thoughts on which tactic to take that will be best effective.

Rounding the corner of the house seeing the front door of the hell hole I storm up the stairs. Tunnel vision is at an all time high at this point.

"*My sister is coming home with me by night's end!" Cole, Richard or Demetri be damned!* Remembering that Jane told me about the tunnel having light and all I had to do was find the knob on the first lantern and turn it all the way on. No surprises when you can see. Walking down the tunnel I can hear some chatter echoing in the chamber towards the end.

"Jane!" I holler as I enter the room but as I scan it she is nowhere to be found. *"How is she not here yet?"*

Erin said "I thought you would never show up! It has been about six hours since I have seen Jane. I was getting worried when I hadn't heard from y'all till about an hour or so ago." when she sent me a text to not shoot you when you came through the door.

"So you're welcome!" Erin smirked

Looking at her with piercing eyes she sees that I am in no mood for antics. Jane should have been here by now seeing as I was snatched in her doorway before I could actually leave on my own free will. Concerned, both of them looked up at me at the same time and Cole shouted *"what about Jane?"*

Thinking to myself *"Like you care enough about her to actually be worried!"* so my one and only response to him is "*I don't know, maybe you should ask your "Father!" Because he has my sister in return for y'all bull shit scheme to get some money and family artifacts!"*

Hearing someone come down the hall has all of us on edge when all of a sudden we see Jane's hand slide into the door and the rest slowly follows. Guessing she was just being cautious after the other times she was down here.

"Where have you been?" Jane cuts her eyes at me and then back to Erin. She asked *"if Cole will be okay and is his health out of the woods."* Erin nods and then before I could get a word in edgewise she practically shushes me and asks for us to leave her alone with her Brother. Hesitant in this situation Erin and I just leave like it was a normal family get

together and we just needed to give the family squabble some space.

As Erin and I head down the tunnel it begins to shake and the ceiling begins to crumble apart. So we catch our balance and begin to run to the entrance hoping that Jane and Cole are okay on their end. We make it to the stairs and begin to climb as we reach the dining room. We dust off and I immediately grab my phone to call Jane to make sure she is okay.

The phone is ringing and of course no response coming from inside the tunnel as Erin hollers for her. Just a loud ringing and smashing noise begins like some type of gigantic grandfather clock is chiming in our ears! Dropping the phone because the sound is unbearable the phone shatters as the ground quakes. Turning to see how Erin is taking all of this and she has disappeared instantly into the tunnel. She screams as she falls, hitting every step on the way down. She fell so fast I didn't have enough time to think about what I just witnessed. The Ground surrounding the tunnel is becoming more and more unstable and the
entrance begins to crumble at my feet. I holler at her as her shadow of a body is glowing. I don't see her move.

"How am I going to get to her without trapping both of us? or Killing both of us?"

I turned to see if maybe I could find something to lower down to her to but with nothing in sight I just agreed to climb down into the hole and retrieve her and just pray to the Gods that we both make it out and she is okay.

Looking around at my immediate surroundings, the entrance is a mess. The doors hinges are all pinched and crippled and the house is shaky like it is ready to swallow us all whole. I turn to begin my descent into the now completely dark abyss and my mind already begins to wonder back to Jane. *"God if I ever get that woman back in my sight I will never let her out of it again."* She seems to leave a wake of chaos in her path lately.

I begin to hear a slight moan below me, but I have only made it about half way down. *"Hold on Erin, I am on my way to get you, be still"* Trying to keep her calm as I order her to listen to me. I continue my way down slowly trying to not disturb any more of the tunnel.

The passageway begins to quake again and this time I have to try to keep my grip on the ledge that is supporting me.

Hoping it doesn't tumble taking me with it to the bottom of the pit with Erin.

"Take Cover" I shout to Erin, as the rocks start coming down almost knocking me off the ledge and I hear her holler in pain. And in the same breath I begin to scream out in anguishing pain wanting to be able to hold on for dear life but my fingers won't hold. and down I go hitting the crumbling steps on my way down. Landing within inches of Erin, I can see her leg bent in a bad position with her tibia sticking out of her skin. The blood coming out of a few places of her body that has already begun to pool underneath her, she turns to me and I black out.

Jane

"How are you and me in this room?" I asked Cole

Because the last I knew, I was in the hall between some rocks, and Cole was handcuffed to the bottom of the bed in that chamber.

"Cole, what is going on?" with both of us confused and not comprehending what is going on, I crawl across the floor till my hand reaches Coles. *"If you try anything sketchy, I will not hesitate to finish the job I started!"*

"Shhh!" Cole says *"I can hear footsteps!"*

We both sit in silence, trying to figure out who is coming down the hall. *"Hopefully it is Bryce and Erin to dig us out of this place."*

The steps stop and the door opens with its eerie noise that will haunt you even in your sleep. A woman in a cloak stands in the entrance of the doorway and her presence causes my skin to burn and tingle in a way that was familiar to when the chime rang in the hall just before I ended up here. She says nothing but commands attention all the same. I glance over at Cole and he is shaking in fear, like he has seen a ghost.

"Cole, are you okay?" I whisper in his direction. He doesn't even bat an eye. *"Cole!"* I scream.

Suddenly the Tingeing burns and a crackling in my skin shows. *"What the hell!"*

The woman interrupts, *"He won't say anything because he knows what he did to me."* I turn to stare at the lady, trying to get a good look at her in the dark, and she takes off her hood from her cloak. The light from the hall glistens around her and for the first time since she appeared I can make out her face.

This woman has a face that I know, her glass blue eyes with the freckles across the bridge of her nose and her cherry red lips that match mine. The wavy hair that has a silver gray tone to it but the wavy messy locks match mine in every other way. *She is standing in front of me like nothing had happened when I knew the truth. I lived it; I know it happened for a fact, so how is it she is standing right here?*

"Mom?" Still in shock, she smiles and points at Cole. *"He owes both of us the truth of what happened,"* she says in a low, angry voice.

I look at Cole still in a daze, not being able to reach him. I rare back and slap him across the face. He blinks and slowly turns his head towards mine. With a tear trickling down his face, he cries out, *"I am so sorry I didn't know!, I didn't know! Please understand everything was a lie until now!"* Grabbing Cole by the shoulders, I shake him to get him to get a grip

"What is she talking about?"

"You know that job I told you Richard roped me into doing for him and his boss? Well, it was to clean up after them when they finished a job. The job at the time, I swear I didn't know, was our mother!"

With an empty stare, I almost look past Cole, when my response just falls out of my mouth without control. *"You monster, I should have just let you bleed out when I shot you!*

How could you condone such horrible behavior, much less be part of it?"

Cole, with severe fear and trepidation, responds with, *"You knew about Richard as much as I did, so how dare you accuse me of condoning such a horrible person!"* Appalled, I lean back and realize *he is right. I knew the type of person Richard was and the kind of people he worked for. I chose not to do anything about it.*

"That makes me just as bad as you," looking him dead in the face as I say those words out loud. Everything goes silent and for a moment, I forget Jessica is standing mere feet from me. Looking up at her with tears in my eyes, *the first thing I want to do is to apologize for the both of us. The second thing is I want to know how she is here now after Cole and Richard did what they did?* But before I could, she shakes her head and says

"Whatever you are thinking, it is unnecessary because we only have a little bit of time before I have to leave."

We both are staring as our mother waves us to come to her at the door. My brain can't filter all the emotions and the current situation at the same time and for a moment, I can't move, think, or even breathe. For a matter of fact I had realized that I was holding my breath and I could hear my heart beating in my ears, which made me gasp out loud. Everything is speeding by even though I am sitting still on the floor.

The burning of my skin begins to intensify, and it is almost like someone is lighting a match and setting me on fire. A low chiming noise is buzzing in my ears, almost like I have a bee flying around my head. Thoughts racing in and out, not being able to finish one without starting another. I close my eyes for a second to focus on the here and now when I feel a flash.

My eyes pop wide open and for a moment I look at Cole, but I'm not sure he saw anything because he was still staring at our mother. *"Cole!"* I yell this time. He just turns his head to stare at me as if I was just a random figure in time, unable to speak.

For years, I had no family and no sense of community other than my work life. Now out of a mere three days I have a mother I never meet other than living her brutal last moments and brother I have known to be a friend '*But has recently tried to kill me to gain something for himself'* and maybe even someone I could care for but with the tunnel collapsing in on itself I am not sure he is even alive.

Cole shoves on my arm to get my attention and out of reflex I elbowed him in the gut.

"Sorry" as he buckles over holding himself, which made me grin just a little. We both stand to our feet and walk over to Jessica as she turns her back to us. A little odd but with both hands she reaches behind her as to have us grab onto hers.

The building lights flicker even though there was no way that they could be functioning after they collapsed when the tunnel crumbled above us. Wind picks up in the room as we hold on to Jessica's hands. Items fly past us as if there is a worm hole sucking everything into it and Jessica is the anchor keeping us still amongst it all.

"What is happening?" Cole hollers over the wind. Something strange occurs. Cole's eyes go black in an instant and his body flickers with the cracks beaming black auras from within. Black smoke consumes the area in which he kneels, not able to control any of the commotion.

The noise echoes as the chiming of a bell gains its strength, and the wind howls in the small chamber. Everything being consumed by some sort of supernatural power. Looking at Cole while he is buckled over on his knees with one hand in Jessica's and the only other free hand on his ear, "*Cole! are you alright?*" Cole screams and I can't move to help. The sound is so horrendous that it takes over the room, causing the walls to come down the louder he yells. The mercy in his voice hurts my soul, as I can't do anything to help. *"Cole!"* I yell again.

He doesn't even hear me through the chaos and smoke as he flickers, like lightning cracking in the dark sky during a hellish storm. The black glow seeping through those very cracks shines like an obsidian after a volcano erupts! Cole begins to scream and shake like he was in immense pain. His skin is now producing an ash like he is about to erupt into flames when suddenly a bright beam of gray and blue light flashes and he disappears!

My eyes widen and I scream in terror, bouncing my eyes between where Cole was crouched down and to where Jessica was standing like nothing was going on.

"Cole!" I holler. The tingling intensifies and the ringing in my ears now has me numb. With everything in slow motion, it is as if I could see everything happening from an out-of-body experience. Looking down at the ground where my one free hand is, it does what I just witnessed Cole go through! The red beam of lights coursing through me sets me on fire. *"Jessica! Please stop!"* Nothing, not even a notion that she heard me the first million times I hollered her name! *This is it, I thought. We both are going to pay for AJ's crimes. We Will both die and not know the reason for which we warranted the death sentence.*

Hollering at Jessica for her to stop doing this, she doesn't flinch at the notion I am trying to free my hand from hers. Impossible as it may seem, it is like my hand is encased in cement that weighs a few tons. Her grip is forever holding and I start to burn just as bright as Cole did.

Did I just watch Jessica kill Cole for what he did to her?

Suddenly, like Cole, a large and bright flash occurs, and just like that, something happens to me. Time slows and I burn, but the sense of it is gone. It's just a flame that is part of me now. I squeeze my eyes shut, not wanting to see what happens to me, but suddenly a hand gets placed on my shoulder as if it was all a dream. No more chiming and tingling, no numb feeling for the overstimulation of pain and to top it all off, no head splitting headache causing a blurred vision. Everything comes into focus now and my eyes widen.

I shift my view from the ground to what is standing in front of me and I am in total shock. *"Am I dead?"* Looking around for Cole and Jessica, but it is only me and this…, this, thing!

"Who are you, and where is this place?"

Looking around, I see four walls covered in a dark mist that extends as far upward as I can see. It creeps along to no end until I turn around. Standing alongside me is a box of some sort, on a pedestal. In my view, just past it, is some kind of entrance that resembles an old clock with a spinning like vortex. There is another person in a hooded cloak. Almost like he is there to guard it or keep someone or thing from coming through. Frightened, I turned to see if it was the same person who grabbed me but he was still standing on the other side of me.

In sheer terror, I ask *"Where am I?"*

Octavia C. Penn

The man in the cloak looks up at me and I can't make anything out besides the glow of his eyes. He responds with a grunt that does not say much, other than this is going to be a lot harder if he says nothing.

"Look, I am not the patient type, so if you can't help me, please point me toward someone who can."

With the man by the portal just standing there as a statue I guess he can't help or won't help either. *I need to get back home because there are people counting on me that are in a lot of trouble.* Feeling like I am giving orders, this man seems to think it is humorous because he seems to voice an echo of a chuckle.

"Where are Cole and Jessica?"

Finally, the man in the cloak takes his hood off and I can't stop staring. He is almost angelic.

But then he opens his mouth and yep… he's a man, ignores my question and starts his own conversation.

"My name is Micheal and you are here to choose" as he points at the Majestic clock looking thing behind me.

"What do you mean, choose?"

"You will need to choose how this story plays out. One path will lead to great power and strength, but the other will lead to great loss and a life of emptiness."

When this situation could be any more confusing, I was wrong. Turning to look at the portal for a second, wondering if what Micheal said has anything to do with this, I throw my eyes back in his direction and he is gone.

"Just like that, I am standing in the room of emptiness with a statue of a, I don't know what, and an angelic clock portal and a box on a pedestal, pissed and bewildered. Now what do I do?"

Turning to look at the box on the pedestal I slowly inch closer and just before I could touch it I hear *"I wouldn't if I were you!"* Turn to see the statue of a person step forward just in time to keep me from touching the box and opening it.

"Oh, now you want to speak!" with a sarcastic tone in my voice, I stare him down with a stern look. He continues to step forward and removes his hood. *"I am just the messenger,"* he answers.

"My name is Gabriel, and you are Jane."

"Well, now that we are introduced, can you please explain to me what I am supposed to be choosing per se?"

Cole and Richard

"I am going to get even with Bryce when I can get my hands on him after Demetri gets what he needs out of him and Jane! No one sucker punches me and gets away with it. I don't care who they are!" Richard yells as he marches his way up the hallway to the stairs to go meet Demetri. Wiping the blood from my mouth, I reach the top of the staircase and I see that Demetri is sitting in the corner that he always sits in. A few of the other men are sitting at the bar having a few drinks and chatting it up like it was a normal Tuesday night.

I walk over to where Demetri is sitting and I casually sit down and pull out a handkerchief out of my suit pocket and place it to my lip. Demetris' reply is somewhat of the humorous kind when he looks to see that I let Bryce get the better of me in the basement.

"Is it done?" he asks Richard in a more serious manner?

"Yes, and I let him walk away thinking he got the better of me because you know I am a good soldier and I follow orders to the T."

"Don't get a smart mouth with me or I will add to the bloody lip you're babysitting over there." Demetri nods and two of his bodyguards stand up and walk over and stand on both sides of me. I slide backwards into my seat and shut my mouth. *"I am not one to take a beating at my age, maybe when I was in my twenties, but not now, so I just shut up and listen."*

"*Now that you are sitting here in front of me I am going to let you know I sent someone to clean up the mess that you and your 'son' have made and you are not to leave out of this room until it's done once and for all."*

"What do you mean by clean?"

"Does he mean clean up the evidence or clean up a problem that didn't get fixed?"

With a worried expression on my face, two hands get placed on my shoulders as they push down to keep me from moving when I hear the words come from Demetris' mouth.

"You know what I mean. I sent one of my cleaners to clean up this whole mess before it goes any further and leads back to me. No thanks to you or Cole. So sit down, shut up and don't move."

A few seconds go by and he looks at me and then asks me if I *"would like something to drink"* as if it was just so casual that he just told me he sent someone to kill Cole. Just as if nothing had just happened, that made me question my line of work. He is so cold, and every move is calculated. Never realizing how unfeeling and detached he or this business could be until it affected me.

I have to find a way to get to Cole and warn him. Looking around at the people that he has in the clubhouse, and to say they are amongst the heavy hitters. *"Who could he have sent?"* Two men at the bar loudly banter with each other as they stare at their phones. They are the usual dumb and dumber. They never leave Demetri's side unless told to. I am almost convinced they share one brain, nothing but muscle. The other three are standing around the pool tables shooting pool and shooting shit with each other just keeping it casual. Everyone is almost accounted for except the scrawny kid that is never around unless Demetri lets him. *"I don't see him being the one to do the job Demetri sent out for."* The two men at the bar then get up and head our way. Guess there is some news to the job that is being carried out as we speak.

Bracing myself for some bad news but they don't say anything aloud for me to hear. They stop just shy of being in front of Demetri and one of them leans into his ear to whisper. Whatever it was, he didn't like it. Demetri's face goes cold and dark as he stares into my soul. He stands up and growls, *"Grab him and follow me now! I am done with this shit!"*

"What now" I holler?

Demetri starts by standing up and chugging his bourbon, followed by throwing his glass against the wall behind him. Shards of glass go flying all over the concrete floor and all the men take cover. Demetri marches toward the front door. Everything is so silent now you could hear a pin drop if need be. He opens the door and hollers get out, not knowing how this is going to end. I try to ask what is going on but the two men aren't taking any of it and they both grab me one on each side and they chunk me out the door like yesterday's garbage.

Landing on every step on the way down, I come to a halt when my body meets the ground, slamming my face into the gravel. Sitting up immediately picking the rocks off my face, the door slams and they disappear inside, leaving me laying in the front drive. *God, please tell me that Cole finished what he was set out to do and if not, I need to get to him, fast or lord help him.*

I stumble to my feet, grabbing the railing of the stairs that led to the doors that they hurled me out of. Beating on them till someone answers so they could at least let me know what happened so that I could at least figure out how bad of a situation Cole and I have made. Looking to the heavens, I pray out loud, hoping he hears me. *"God, please let Cole be okay. He is just doing what I had asked him to do. For him to fix what AJ and I had started and couldn't finish."*

"Condemn me, not him."

I was just trying to give him a way in and he screwed it up.

Beating vigorously on the door and screaming for Demetri to let me in until my hand begins to throb and bleed, but I am wasting precious time and no answer from anyone inside. Standing there on the top step of the stoop, I hear the engines of a few of the vehicles that escort Demetri around start up. Doors slam shut one by one. I hurry down the step and make my way to the edge of the building when I see two blacked out vans and Demetri's car make their way out of the garage. One van in front and the other behind to follow always in the middle is Demetri, so that he keeps on guard from his enemies.

Waiting for them to get to the end of the drive, I head inside through the back door from the garage as the door shuts. *"This is my only chance to grab a vehicle and try to make it there before they can do anything to Cole."*

I have to stop them.

Grabbing a set of keys that are hanging on the wall, I hear a walkies-talkie go off in the back of the room. Jumping, I drop the keys and squat down in case some person sees me. A few seconds go by and I realize some idiot left theirs sitting on the dock, leaving the power on. I scramble across the floor looking like a deranged monkey to grab it and I can hear their whole conversation.

"Tonight they all die!" The voice is Demetri's, and he seems irritated. *"I've had enough of the games and this needs to be ended before the other families find out and come for me."*

"This is coming straight down from the head of the families!"

Another man on the other end of the conversation just replies back with a *"Yes sir"* and the talkies go silent.

"Coming from the head of the 'Families'? I thought Demetri was the head? What is going on here?"

"That is my cue" thinking about my next moves and how I need to execute them without getting Cole or myself killed. I press the key on the button fob to see what car I swiped and ran over to get into it. Cranking it up, I press the garage door opener. Out of nowhere near the back, a door opens, and a big pissed off burly man enters the garage and screams, *"Hey you're not supposed to be in here!"* That was my cue. I hit the gas and barrel through the slowly opening garage door like it was made of paper.

"Only a few dents to the hood and a small crack to the windshield as it clipped the bottom of the door, so in all I believe I will make it to my destination without delay!"

Octavia C. Penn

Speeding down the drive and I make it to the street and a few of Demetri's goons are standing in the drive of the property holding me at gunpoint, screaming to stop and to get out. *"Man, at this point, manslaughter or murder is not a good option."*

With my foot on the brake, I test their loyalty by revving the engine, letting them know I will run them down if need be.

I grab the talkie that I threw in the passenger seat and I get Demetri's attention. *"Demetri, I have your precious car in front of your warehouse and I will burn it all down if you don't turn around and leave my kid alone."*

A pause over the radio, and then I hear *"You burn it down! That will seal his and your fate! What do you expect me to do after this fuck up went south?"*

With silence on both ends of the Radio I blurted out, *"I mean It I will burn it all down. You have kids yourself. You know what lengths you will go in order to protect them. Don't Test me!"*

With a quick response, I ask him in a begging manner to *"let me handle the situation. You come back here so let me do this! I will get this done. You can even send someone to watch the house, just in case."*

The silence over the radio seems like for an eternity before I get a response. The men that had the car surrounded are now slowly moving out of the way as to give me the all clear.

Pulling forward slowly, I hear screeching tires come from around the corner and I meet them head on in the driveway. First, a black van pretty much parks bumper to bumper to the car that I have stolen and waits. Followed around the corner was Demetri's car. It pulls up just next to mine and a window rolls down. *"You better get this done. This is your only second chance!"*

He waves the driver forward and continues to say, *"You have balls to threaten me. Don't ever think you will get away with trying to take what's mine from me again? You won't walk away!"*

"Now get out of my car and get in the van with them!" Nodding in the men's direction that parked in front of me to block the car, the side door slams open and a man gets out. *"They will take you to the house and bring you back when or if you do what you were told. And if you don't come*

back, that's not really a concern to me either way! I meant it when I said I was done with you!"

Demetri's car pulls off towards the garage that I had just barreled through and the man that got out of the van walks over and opens the door. He motions for me to get out. Slowly I slide out of the car and make a wide berth to the van door and he shoves me in without hesitation *"We don't have all day Grandpa! Let's get this over with!"*

Bryce

"*Bryce!, Bryce, please open your eyes!*" Rocks bouncing off the floor left and right of us like a pinball game, and we are the levers. Erin's voice echoes in my ears as my head pounds from the fall that ended with my body coming to an abrupt stop when it slammed against the floor. The room is dark and only with the feeling of my hands around me can I feel the amount of blood on the floor seeping from Erin's body. She will not last much longer if I can't get us out of here.

With no hope of getting us both out of here because of her condition and my lack of ability to carry her up the cliff. Both suffering injuries to the body with hers life threatening. I turn to get her attention.

"Erin, how do you feel?" Thinking about how *that is a dumb question to ask someone in her predicament, but I want to get her mind off of the fact she isn't going to make it out of her alive.*

"I can't feel my body, Bryce!" Taking my hand and placing it on her arm, she is cold and shivering. Her voice was so soft and fragile, she stuttered out the sentence "*Please tell my loved ones I love them. Please, if you get out of here, please don't leave my body here alone! I don't want to be alone or forgotten, promise me you will get me!"*

I just lay there and hold her hand, hoping it brings her some kind of comfort in this hell, not knowing exactly what to say. Listening to the sound of her sobbing in the dark, I asked her a question, "*Why did you agree to help Jane? Why put yourself in harm's way if knowing what she asked you to do was dangerous?"*

Without hesitation she responds, "*When someone risks their livelihood to help a friend without asking, the least I could do is return the favor when needed."* Wondering what she meant, she didn't even miss a beat and continued to tell me.*Last year, I was in a relationship with a man that I thought I was going to spend the rest of my life with. Everything was great, we were looking at apartments to rent together, talking about our future and kids, he even asked me to marry him. When one day he came over and he was drunk and pissed from being fired from work. He had been out at the bar all afternoon and had time to stew on the day. So when he showed up, he took the problem out on my face and stomach with an aluminum bat that I kept by the front door for my protection. When I made it to the room, I locked the door, and I made a panicked call to Jane for help and the whole time she stayed on the phone with me, listening to the monster on the other end of the phone. She rushed to my aid. The whole time*

she heard me screaming in pain and for help. He busted through the door as I hid the phone from him under the bed and he beat me so badly I thought I was going to die. When I heard her bust through the front door, he stopped hitting me and went to confront Jane, but she had her gun ready and waiting for him to show himself. She held him at gunpoint and threatened to shoot him if he moved and not a minute later, the police and ambulances showed up and it was all over.

Without asking, she went to the hospital to stay with me and to make sure I was okay and I will always be in her debt and whenever she called it was my way to return a favor for a friend. No questions asked. That is how our friendship has worked. From the start, I wouldn't trade it for nothing."

Erin coughs. It is the sound of nightmares; It sounds like she is drowning in her blood and I when she breathes in; she is aspirating everything that she coughs up. I scoot close to her and attempt to turn her on her side but she hollers as I move her, "*Stop! For the love of god please, leave me!"*

My heart breaks for her as she slips away, her breathing getting shallower, and I start to holler for help, hoping someone would hear us and send for some help. Hoping that someone has heard the building crumbling and has called for someone to do a well check on it but, *that seems like a lot of hoping and nothing getting done.*

"***Help!***" I scream at the top of my lungs. ***"Help!"***

Taking a break from the screaming, I notice my voice is the only one making any noise. The silence breaks me and tears begin to well up in my eyes and my throat comes to a knot when I swallow.

"*Erin*?"

"Erin? Please say something. I don't want to be alone down here. Please, Erin!"

The silence is insurmountable and the tears are now free, falling harder than I have ever cried as a grown man. Realizing that I am still holding on to Erin's hand, I slowly let go as I said to her as if she could hear me, "*I won't leave you here, I promise!*" The ground begins to shake and crack beneath me as I force myself to move quickly to the same side that Erin's body is laying and a hole opens, engulfing the surrounding floor as if something swallowed it whole.

At that time I hear a familiar voice from up above and it is one that I would rather it not be, but at this point beggars can't be choosers. The voice hollers into the Chasm as I look up. My eyes meet Richards as he hollers for Cole.

"Cole!"

His voice seems shaky as he probably thinks that I am the body that is shifting in a panic on the chasm floor. I holler at the top of my lungs, *"Help! The floor is falling out from beneath us and it's crumbling fast!"* Richard hollers, *who is "Us!"*

"*It is Bryce and Erin, Cole and Jane are at the other end of the tunnel and we haven't heard from them. Last I saw of them, they were in the dungeon at the other end when the tunnel began to collapse!"*

Hoping that Richard stays to help instead of leaving me to rot down here after I sucker punched him.

I hoped too soon because just as I finished the sentence, his head disappeared from the hole in the dining room floor and we were left alone once again.

"Richard? Please, Richard, we need your help!"

A few minutes go by and a strand of sheets tied together falls over the edge of the hole and hits the floor. Richard demands, *"Wrap it around you and I'll pull you up!"*

"I need you to get Erin first!" Hollering up to Richard. *"I promised I wouldn't leave her down here!"*

Richard hollers back in a loud growl, *"Hurry! The ground is giving way minute by minute, so you better do whatever you need to do so that we all three make it."*

Grabbing the Sheets and sliding it under Erin, tying it around her chest like it is a vest and holler *"Pull her up Richard!"* Watching him lift her up, I hold her head from hitting up against the rocks. *"Be careful"* I screamed. Watching her body lift out of sight, the real panic sets in. *I hope that he hurries and gets the sheets back down here before the ground disappears into nothing. But at the same time secretly hoping he falls in after I get out of here, he has the nerve to be here after everything they have done. It is going to be a cold day in hell before I could ever have any respect for Jane's new found brother or his 'father'.*

The sheets get thrown back over and I follow the same procedure. I tie it around me under my arms and knot it around my chest. Richard pulls me up as I dangle. He is beginning to struggle. I slide down the side of the wall and then he gets me another four feet and I slide again. *"The tug of war with gravity is causing the hole to widen!"* Richard grunts.

The air tastes like it is full of iron and it is gritty as I inhale it as it falls around my face. I can see Richard sliding forward from the gravel, being loose beneath his feet. As I bare down to grit my teeth, I bite into the dirt, making this loud popping noise in my ears. Not thinking about how I am trying to help climb out of here all busted up. But with every flex of muscle on my body, it sends a pounding to my head, making my vision go blurry. I can now hear Richard like I am standing just inches from him. I glance up and see him reaching for my hand and I take it. Letting go of the sheets, he grabs me by the wrists and pulls me above the ledge and over to the ground. We both roll out of death's way as the side disappears from sight, both taking a second to catch our breath.

"*The house is about to come down! We better get out of here!*" Richard screams as some beams begin to fall. Moving just fast enough to miss one of them falling, I almost fell back into the pit.

"*We have to get Jane!*" Staring down Richard like a menace waiting for him to say the wrong response so I could shove his ass in and call it a day. But he hollers that he knows another entrance into the tunnels and to follow him.

"*We can't leave Erin!*" They both grab her limbs on each end of her and firefighter tote her out of the building. Making it to the curb outside, we sit Erin on the ground carefully and I tell Richard, "*stay here and to call emergency services.*"

Richard has other things on his mind and doesn't hesitate to just drop her and run in the opposite direction. "*Fuck! Richard, you're a fucking prick, always out for yourself. Be damned who gets in the way!*" Richard never missed a step, and the night swallows him like he never existed.

Cole and Richard

Screaming laying on the ground with both hands over my ears, with my eyes shut and breathing in a lingering toxic air that has me suffocating on the stale smell that has permeated my lungs. *"I am going to die!"* Repeating to myself. I don't know how long I was actually laying there on the ground when I noticed the silence. I opened my eyes slowly as to save myself if something was to kill me as soon as I saw it. "*Kind of like when a child is scared at night in their bed. They hide under the covers with their eyes shut, thinking that the covers are magical and can save them from the monsters."*

This place is such a dark area, but everything glows like it has a backlight. It outlines the details of the place in

which I woke up in. Looking around the vast emptiness, I don't see Jane anywhere. Studying
my surroundings to see where Jessica zapped me to, but nothing is familiar.

Everything echoes with each movement of my body and suddenly I hear, "*Don't move.*" The voice is such an intense, low growl that every sense in my body gets heightened.

"*Who said that?*" my voice trembling with uncertainty. *No matter where I look to move to, there is no escaping, there is nowhere to hide!* When out of the dark, a shadowed figure emerges and stands roughly eight feet from me.

"*My name is Azrael,*" He sternly bellows. "*You are in purgatory, but unlike your sister, you share a less favorable fate. This fate is going to be met no matter the course, but who is standing alongside you is your choice in the end.*"

Staring at this man in all black with clear eyes and a hooded cloak, he carries a blade the length of his own body.

"Azrael, as in The Angel of Death?" I thought that was all talk and no substance, boy was I wrong.

"Why am I here?"

"How do I get out of this place?"

"Where is Jane?"

With a disgruntled growl, Azrael Screams

*"**Enough**!"*

"The only way you get out of here is if you truly understand your sins and why your fate is less favored. For if you don't accept this, you will be stuck here for eternity." Azrael turns to face the distance abyss and takes one area and makes a wide waving motion. And like everything in this place, a giant black and red portal opens up.

Shell-shocked and at the same time mesmerized by the size and detail of this object, I walked towards it and then remembered that *I was told specifically not to move by the Angel of Death himself.*

like a child, I sort of raised my hand to interrupt Azrael and ask him "*if it is okay if I were to follow him over to the portal."*

Waving his blade at me, signaling that it was okay, he pointed me to an altar with a box upon it. This box is black and has a thorn vine like wire etched into it that wraps it up almost like barbed wire. The gold vine shimmers against the dark that surrounds it like it is calling to me. The closer I move towards it, the louder a bee-like humming emerges and takes over. It's almost like I am hypnotized and have no control as it pulls me in.

Standing side by side with Azrael and a box in which I have no clue what it holds frightens me. Eager to see what is inside, I place my hand on it, causing a jolt of energy to rush through my veins. Intending to open it myself, Azrael slams his arms against my body, shifting me so much I lose my balance and fall to my ass.

"*You don't even know what this is and you want to touch it or even open it?*"

"*Greed and Gluttony have definitely ruled the earth more than any of us have paid attention to. And you humans always want what you can't or should not have!*" The tone that is coming from Azrael has my full attention.

You mortals don't even think about what it would do to others. As long as you are doing it for yourself, the rest of the world be damned!"

Azrael seemed peeved and the look that he was giving me could have and most definitely should have killed me. His eyes glowed immensely and out of control. He threw his cloak off and what was hidden underneath his robe shot out were these large black and silver feathered wings that looked torn and tethered all over besides the majority of the tips that were razor sharp.

"*Point taken!*" I shout as I turn to run behind the altar to hide just in case he decides I am done for and not worth his time.

"*You idiot,* he growls, *this is Pandora's Box. This is what I needed to tell you before you unleashed hell on earth.*"

My eyes widen and my full attention shifts from Azrael to the Box. Sliding out from behind the altar and he continues.

"*Are you ready to listen to me now or are you ready to move on to your fate without knowing how to maneuver the outcome in your favor?*"

Shaking my head in compliance and shutting my mouth so that I don't step on his last nerve, I stand up to be somewhat level with him.

"This man is all of seven feet tall with black hair down past his shoulders and the body of a football god!" A quick chuckle and then back to reality, sort of.

"*Are you paying attention?"* Azrael asks.

The quickest "*Yes*!" flies out of my mouth, followed by nothing but silence.

"*Good, your life has never been in your own hands and The Sisters of Fate has it already sealed, so if you would like to have some sort of control over how you meet your end, I need you to hear me."* Azrael is nodding in my direction, almost like he is trying to convince me to do as he says.

When your sister was born, you weren't even a thought in time or space. Your sister was already given a divine path and when your father AJ sold her on the black market, little did he know it was to a group of demons that run the Chicago city area.

Azazel and his men took that child and pawned her off to a family that was supposed to raise her till she came into her powers. But the night that you were born, the fates turned, and they died before they should have. Again Jessica was so grief stricken that she couldn't keep you and with the feeling of rejection, it stained your soul and sent you down a dark path separate to your sisters.

When you were born, it caused a cataclysmic event that made the world shift on its axis. It made the rainfall from the heavens freeze the world till your mother was done delivering you. That is what ultimately killed your sisters' parents. This is what charged her powers before she knew she had them.

Those nights that you can't remember after your mother died growing up was a stress induced charge. See, I have been watching you since you were young and when you are placed in a hard position that has a lot of emotion tethered to it; you go dark.

Azrael Grabs my arm and my eyes cloud over black. Next thing I see is the moment that my mother is on her deathbed and I am sitting at her bedside. It is almost as if I am here reliving the moment all over again. The sounds of the monitors that are beeping and the oxygen pumping through the tube into her body are so loud that it takes over my senses. As I listen to the whistle of the air push through the small canal, Azrael places a tighter grip on me. Searing his print into my arm, then lifting it away as I rip free from his grip.

"What the hell was that for?" shifting to the side to step away from him as I rub the mark that is now permanently burned into my skin. The smell takes me out of the room for a moment in time and then with a hum of a flat line I am instantly back. Watching my mother die all over again and knowing that I can't do shit is traumatizing. I stand there watching as that innocent boy grieves the mother that he loved so dearly.

"You are now tethered to me, Azrael says, and whenever I need you, It will locate you and you will be brought to me."

Now watch what happens next. Azrael tells me to watch as if I didn't live through it. *"I know what happened. I don't need to see this unless this is your way of torturing me!"* I grunted in a low but hurt voice. The tears welled up, as if I could help it at all. *"This woman is the person I called mom for my entire life and through some cruel twist of fate she dies so that I can become some monster?"*

"No, thanks I'll pass!" shrugging my shoulder in the opposite direction of the dark shadowed man. Azrael grabs a hold of me and before I could stop him, we were back in that dark place between the living and hell.

"What do you mean, 'suit yourself?' As if I have a choice."

"You die and your mother's life meant nothing and her dying was all in vain or you take what I am offering you and you die and you do something about the people and the fates that gave you a shitty life. I am offering you a seat at my table, one where you have a small say in how you live the rest of your eternity."

"There is a catch to this and you must accept this or it is a no go for getting your 'slice of pie,' so to speak."

"What is it?" I ask.

You must finish what Richard sent you to do. You must finish off your sister so that she can't stop our plans for earth.

Can I really do that? I ask myself. *Given the fact that I had just done this very thing or at least attempted it makes me believe even more that Azrael is right: I have no choice and this will play out either way. At least with all the chess pieces on the board, I can control the outcome in my favor.*

I look Azrael in the face and nod that I will do as I was just ordered. *"Hell, I just traded one mob for a celestial one is the way I see it."*

The chiming sounds, and I look at Azrael as he hands me a ring: he says this is a talisman that tethers you to my world. This is how the demons in your world will know you are now my property. Now don't waste any more time. You have little of it left.

The chiming is now at an all time pitching high in my ears and my vision fades into a blur. Dropping back down to my knees out of the sheer pain of the intensity of the sound, my skin begins to crack and burn. Just like last time, Beams of dark light flash and I am now laying on the floor of the dungeon that I started this nightmare in.

Second guessing what just happened, I look around to see if Erin or Jane were here. Seeing if they decided to dose me with some pain meds that made me slip into one hell of a dream state, but I was alone.

Moving to push myself up in a seated position, I scratch my arm along the wall when I realize my arm was burned. Searching for a phone along the floor, I finally find what I believe was Janes. Turning the flashlight mode on, I shined it on myself.

"*Holly shit, it was real!*" looking at a hand print that is twice the size of my hand in a burned red color outlined in a stained soft blue as if it was glowing like the glow from an angel. My mouth drops open in disbelief when I hear a faint sound coming from outside the room.

"*Cole, Cole answer me!*" It is Richard and boy, am I happy to hear his voice? "***Help!***" I holler as he gets closer to the room. Richard bust through the door and doesn't hesitate to ask, "*Where is Jane?*"

Jane

Standing there just watching my every move, I holler at him, "*Gabriel! What am I supposed to be choosing?*"

"You are supposed to choose between you and the rest of humanity or choose your brother over it all."

Staring me dead in the face with the most serious look I could imagine he could give, he explains the entire scenario of my birth through adulthood that has led here. *This is apparently my destiny and if it wasn't for AJ and Jessica having a second child, I wouldn't have to choose at all.* The circumstances that surrounded our births started a domino effect.

"So now you are telling me that even though I have never had any siblings and now that I do, I have to choose between myself and all of humanity or to kill him? I won't do it. Cole is my brother, good or not! Besides, don't you all say that we get to choose our destiny? "

"You do get to choose your destiny, but this is fate and whether or not you choose to kill Cole or not he is going to come for you and it will be you against him. You will have to choose. The future of the world is in your hands."

My face goes numb with a blank stare as Gabriel says more than I want him to. He waits for my response and I don't..; I say nothing. I turn to catch my breath before I lose it in front of him and as I turn; I burst into silent tears. Throwing my hands into my face to smother the sound, Gabriel clears his throat and says, "*The box is yours, but before you open it, you need to choose what you are going to do."*

Beginning to get irritated with the situation of having to make some major life alterations in a short period of time I burst like someone dropping mentos in a coke bottle. *"Why can't you just be the one to tell me what it is, you would like me to do because I obviously don't have a choice? Remember, it is fate that has me here!"* His body shift backwards and I just can't stop myself after being brutally tortured and raped and belittled by maniac monsters in ski masks, I keep yelling and let it all out of my system. "*Don't act all surprised that I am this way. You all knew this was coming and you want a normal, everyday person to fix your problems!"*

"*Jane*!" A loud voice appears behind me *"Gabriel you can let me take care of this!"* It is Jessica, she is standing right in front of me but this time she isn't in a cloak and I can't imagine her being any more beautiful than she is right now.

Jessica Standing in front of me with no bruises or a bullet hole in her head with no marks on her at all and I can see that for myself. She has gray hair, blue eyes and a beaming glow to her whole self. She walks around me to the box on the pedestal and picks it up. Not before I notice the long white and fluffed feathers that are hanging to the ground from her back. They are magical and seem to be so many different shades of white that they have a hint of every color hidden within them.

"*Jane, this is our family heirloom that until now, we had to make sure that you would choose the right path before you got it. I believe you found the key to the box hidden in my home?* "

Nodding yes and still in shock, she hands the box to me. As soon as I reached for the box that she grips tightly, Jessica asks me "*to please make the right choice because she can no longer do this job anymore.*" Confused as to what she is talking about when she mentions she can't do it any longer, I asked "*What job was that?*"

"*I am a* Phoenix." her eyes narrow in on mine as we make contact and she continues to convince me of what she is. Her wings widen almost double her length. "*When you get the key and open this box, you will find the artifact. You will need to put it on. It will activate your powers at full force, causing mine to drain because there can only be one of us at a time. You will take my place and you will have to carry out the duties you were born with. Just know that I have always loved you and no matter what happens, you are my child.*"

Jessica's eyes fill with tears and as she closes her eyes, the floodgates open. Jessica steps forward and opens her arms in which I feel like I need to embrace and I do. "*What will happen to you after I consume the total power of the Phoenix?*"

Octavia C. Penn

"I become human and I live as long as I can, My time on earth was always meant to bring you here to this moment. You are my greatest accomplishment" I smile, knowing that something good has come from this and she gets to have a happy ever after on earth, a do over of sorts. Our embrace ends and Jessica instantly disappears from my sight.

Looking at the box in my hand that holds my future, I grip it tight. Scanning my surroundings, I holler for Micheal and for Gabriel, hoping one of them could point me toward my new fate. I holler, and holler and holler, and no answer, so I get a bit more nosy and I walk on over to the portal that is swirling in front of me.

Here we go not long after I decide that I am going to snoop. The ground shakes and the room fills with a dark mist as I get closer to the vortex in the portal. Walking up the steps, I can make an image out in the center of the portal. "*It is Cole and Richard. They are in the tunnel under Jessica's home. What are they arguing about?*" My skin begins to tingle and burn the more I focus in on them. When suddenly I feel a hand on my shoulder just like before and when I turn around, I see him. It is Micheal standing there with his smug grin upon his face and with his witty line of *"Sorry I was late to the party but I'm here now."* He places his gigantic hand on my shoulder and a hot glow sears my skin. "*Get your hands off me! What the hell are you trying to do, kill me?"*

Micheal grins and his voice breaks its calm sound with a bad boy reaction "*not yet we aren't!"* and with the last syllable leaving his breath he shoves me into the portal.

Landing on the Ground skidding face first across it like I was stealing third base, I lost control of the box from Jessica and my anger all in one. "*That angel is a piece of work! Wait till I see him again.*" The room hasn't changed any from the last time I was in it, other than I am alone now. Scrambling to get to the box that launched itself from my arms when I landed on the hard ground, I hear Cole and Richard's voice waning in the distance.

Wanting to get his attention as fast as possible, I just stand up and scream to the top of my lungs, "*Cole*!" the tunnel falls silent and I hear footsteps pitter patter towards me!

"*Jane! where were you and are you okay?"* Weary of his intentions, I plant my feet accordingly and wait for the moment that Gabriel told me would arise.

"*I am back in this horrid room that Jessica zapped us out of. Are you okay?"* Asking and waiting for his response, he burst through the door and I stood fast. We both pause, eyes gleaming in an unsure manner when he says "*Where did you come from?*"

"Me? You disappeared into thin air in the middle of screaming for your life and now you act as if you are okay? Cole, what is going on?" I demanded he tell me.

His witty response "*and you? Because when I got back, no one was in that room now. You stand here in a ready stance like your life depends on it!*"

With the most serious face I could muster without causing him to react, I lied. I tell Cole that "*Jessica zapped me to some room and that it only seemed to be for a few seconds, then I ended up back here in this dungeon like nothing had happened. When I landed on the ground, I could hear your voice, so I hollered for you just in case they hurt you.*"

Cole's face drops with an icy cold chill that I have only seen on one other person's face before. The man that attacked me upstairs in the house just before I got him in handcuffs. *"That's not good"* , thinking to myself. I ask "*What's wrong?*" About that time the room shakes and Cole's eyes go dark, but this time it seems different. He has control over the force that is consuming him whole. Almost like he is enjoying it more than he should.

I turn to angle my head in a different direction out of view of Cole, so he can't see me as my defenses take their own control over my body like some kind of security system. My eyes gain a sharp focus on everything I intend to focus on and my body begins to glow and burn as a defense to Cole's attempt to harm me.

Thinking *"Jessica didn't warn me that Cole would have powers, and that is how he forces me to choose between him or myself."*

In my thoughts for too long and I get hit by a charge of light that knocks me off my feet and back into the bed that I was standing merely a few feet in front of. Grabbing my side, smelling my singed flesh, I get frantic and realize the box that has the heirloom that is supposed to give me my full power is open on the floor. With each flash of power from Cole, I dart it lights up the room.

"There I see the ring!"

Scrambling to get to it, I slide the ring on my finger. The chiming returns and smoke fills the room just this time faster than I saw in the hall when Gabriel and Micheal told me

I had to choose. The ring slides onto my finger like it was meant just for me and, just like that; the room disappears, along with Cole. The sound is still there but in slow motion and now my body stiffens and I am on my tiptoes like I am being stretched to my ends. The tingling intensifies and my skin bursts into flames; the heat rushing over my body is so intense I almost pass out from the pain. The room spins out of control and then drops me to the floor on my hands and knees. My body trembles and pours sweat off my skin like someone drenched me with a water hose. My life flashes before my eyes and the room comes back into focus when Cole starts to charge at me.

"Cole! Stop! You don't know what you are doing!"

"Like hell I don't!" he shouts as he heads in my direction with anger consuming his rage.

With a quick raise of my hand and a thought of just protecting myself against who is supposed to be my Brother a blast of light emerges from my hand and Cole goes up against the wall and slides down, slamming against the floor. "*Cole, just stop and talk to me. We can figure out what to do that keeps both of us alive!"*

Cole wipes the blood from his lips and looks in my direction.

"So you lied?"

"You do know what has to be done!"

"Where did you get sent to?"

"Because it seems to me like you are choosing the same path I am taking! You're choosing yourself, Jane!" Cole shoots one question after another without letting me respond

"What Just like you? No! I am trying to find a middle ground, but you're not giving me any choice when you attacked me!"

Bryce

Frantic and with my nerves shot, I need to wait for emergency services to arrive, but I can't stick around. If I was to stay and wait for them, I won't be able to get away and make sure Jane is safe from Richard or her brother. So when I hear the sirens near the house, I get up and limp as fast as I can toward where I last seen Richard disappear.

It was a little too late because he was gone in the night before I could follow so now it is a mystery to where he went in at. Sliding out of the sight of the ambulance, I stop and look around, using my wits and years of being a detective to good use and I look around and notice all the houses have lights on except one and the front gate is wide open. *It would make perfect sense for Richard to go in here considering the house is the only one boarded up besides the door.* With the other being one that has a for sale sign on the front stoop that seems warm and inviting even in the dark gleaming around it. *That can't be it too much traffic for a hideout.*

Looking around and turning my thoughts into thinking like a criminal or at the very least a shady person asking myself *"Where did he go in at?"* Also *"What if he is waiting for me around some corner and tries to take me out before I could get in there and help Jane and catch Cole."*

A large and loud sound comes from behind the house just as I attempt to walk up the front stairs. Sounds almost like someone slamming shut a storm cellar door. curiosity sends me quickly hobbling around the back of the house to find a basement door that is half open. As if someone didn't care with the other half of the door being closed because they were in a hurry.

Reaching down to grab onto the railing to help myself down the old wooden stairs and Richard hits me over the head and as I fall, he yanks me backwards onto the ground and gets on top of me.

"*Not yet, you don't*," Richard growled. "*You remember the sucker punch at the warehouse? Well, I do!*" He follows the sentence with a blow to the face. "*Demetri isn't here to keep me from beating your ass!*" With both arms covering my face he keeps pounding me like we were in a schoolyard fight. Rocking to one side, I knock Richard off his balance and I take one leg to wrap it around the front of his body and slam him to the ground. Richard grabs his head with both of his hands, giving me the opportunity to get the upper hand and boy will I.

Standing up and hovering over the top half of his body, I rare back and go to kick him, but the ground shakes, and it causes me to tumble. And just like that, I am once again on my back. Richard is scrambling around to get to his feet but with the chaos, he can only get to his knees and crawls to the entrance of the basement. He gets there and looks back at me just to give me the finger and hollers, "*If I were you I would worry about your sister, not Jane,*" and in he goes closing the door behind him. I follow him to the door but see just as fast that the coward had locked the door behind himself.

I know nothing about this house. I have to help Jane, but Richard is right about Kelcey. I need to find a different way to help her get away from Demetri before he finds out how this evening is going.

Hoping that he doesn't think she is not worth the headache and gets rid of her before I get there. He sent his goons to watch the house and, with all the chaos, I am sure they have already made their way back to report to him.

With a hard decision to make, I saved Kelcey and hope that Jane can hold off Cole and Richard while I send help. Looking around, I see a black car like the one that Demetri's goons drive him around in. I cautiously walk towards it and a man rolls the window down before I could signal.

"*Get in,*" he says "*I saw what happened and don't worry I don't like Richard any more than the next guy, I will help you.*" with what I could only imagine was a shocked look on my face I grunted "*Take me to my sister*."

With complete disbelief in how charming this guy was, he said "*Sure*" just as fast as I demanded. Getting into the back seat of the car, he goes to drive off and, with the other hand, rolls the window up and says, "*Didn't think you wanted to be around when Azazel torched the place.*" Like it was nothing to just admit to committing murder to the Chief of Detectives like we worked together and I wouldn't turn him in.

"*No, what are you doing? Jane is still in there and I need to get her out*!"

"*Sorry boss's orders,*" he barks nonchalantly and locks the doors of the car. "*Demetri told you that you would pay if he didn't get what he was after. Richard and Cole couldn't get it done so with them all three in the house and no way out this is the best solution.*"

"What do I say to this man?" Looking in the window behind me before we turn the corner, I see a man toss a red gas can and start the fire at the house.

"*Let me out now! This was not the deal!*"

"I was supposed to get the artifact and money for him. Demetri was supposed to let me get this done and free my sister and Jane would be okay!" The flames gain height as we gain distance as the house fades when we turn the street corner. "*I will kill all of you!*"

Octavia C. Penn

"Oh, I was supposed to let you know about your friend that died. They picked her up off of the ground where you left her. If you don't comply, we have the video footage that will make it look like you killed her and then ran."

"You bastard! That isn't what happened and you know it!" No response comes from the front of the car and I sit and contemplate my choices.

"How am I going to get Kelcey out of the basement dungeon that they have her locked in?"

COLE AND RICHARD

Shutting the door behind me after having to crawl on my hands and knees to even get in the basement to get away from Bryce is a task in itself. Taking a deep breath as I hurry to lock the latch behind me so he can't follow me in to stop me from having to kill Jane. I listen to him holler from a distance, calling me "*a fucking prick*". The Ground surrounding the entrance at this end of the tunnel was already in shambles so now that the tunnel is collapsing nothing looks the same. There are fallen beams all around the room and concrete cracked as the ground shifts as it gives way to the pressure of the foundation shifting. *The Air in this house is damp and smells like mildew on a good day and now that all of it is coming down all I want to do is get Cole and get out of here. Never looking back at this part of our lives again.*

I am squinting to see the hatch in the floor and it is partially covered by debris. Grabbing the heavy items off the top I struggle to move it. Next the house begins to shake and crumble more around me and in the midst of it all I hear Cole holler on the top of his lungs.

"*I'm coming Cole , hang on!*" I shout above all the noise taking place Reaching down with all my might I lift up on the trapped door and pull it open. The makeshift ladder that is leading its way down to the tunnel is barely holding on to the hinges that keep it up. Looking around before I go in I notice that there is an unusual amount of dust floating around, I pause for just a moment and I see an ominous glow above me in the main house. *"It's smoke!"*

"Bryce is crazy enough he set the house on fire!"

"*Cole*!" I shouted, "*Cole hurry and get up here*!"

With no response, *"I don't think he can hear me, I have to get him."*

Thinking to myself *"I owe him that much after everything that has happened."* Pulling on the door that is already heavy to move when there isn't an excess amount of debris on it but now I can't get it open. I keep hollering in hopes that Cole can hear me. "*Cole*!" About that time I feel the door give way to me as I sit back on my ass while pulling on it. "*There we go I can get it open now"* screaming in a strained voice as the door lifts up over the pivot point and it slams down on the ground wide open. A wave of dust flies up in my face and fills the room to a point of being unable to see more than a foot in front of my face. "*Cole, for the love of god answer me!*" I hear Cole scream on the top of his lungs out of pain. Struggling to see into the hole I just blindly grab on to the ladder and lower myself down one step at a time. The house begins to give way and the ladder falls apart with me on it. With a rough landing I twist my ankle as I land on the bottom darting out of the way of the falling pieces.

The tunnel has shifted so much so that I have to get on all fours and crawl. I slowly inch my way around all the rubble and large debris that has fallen when I meet a pile of rock in my way. *I am going to have to move all this out of my way to make it to Cole. "Damn it this is going to take awhile"* grunting in anger as I grab the top rock and start to push. I noticed that there is space behind it to shove the top out of the way. *Maybe I could just move the top and squeeze through, cutting the time in half. Whatever I do I need to hurry because the house above us is on fire and I won't have much time to persuade Cole to choose himself over Jane!*

Pausing for just a moment to catch my breath I notice that the tunnel is absolutely quiet. You can hear the wind and fire blazing above us. Hoping I get through any minute now. Elbows are bleeding from having to crawl low and it is leaving a trail on everything I pass and touch. "*At least I will find my way back through just having to follow the red brick road*" saying to myself, finding the least bit of humor in this situation will keep me from losing my shit as I force my way down the tunnel.

There I can finally get through, being able to stand when the tunnel shakes violently more times. Just this time I hear Cole over it all. Quickly getting to my feet I run towards the sound and I meet Cole at the door of this Dungeon.

"*What is going on?*" I ask Cole.

Staring him down I notice he is covered in an ash like substance that is floating around him like he just walked out of a fire pit. His skin is glowing a strange glow in these cracks and crevices that are closing up right in front of my eyes. Again I grab Cole by the arms and shake him. Demanding he tell me what happened. But shaking him does nothing and It takes him a few seconds to gather himself then he pushes me away from him.

"You sorry piece of shit! You knew what was going to happen didn't you, and don't lie to me anymore because I know!" A lot has happened since you left me at the basement doorway. Cole's rage makes these ominous black veins reappear.

I pleaded with Cole to tell me everything. "*Where is Jane*!" I demanded. "*Why, now you want to take care of your mess now that it is out of control?"* Throwing my arms up and away from him Richard just stares at me not knowing how to respond. I push past him and attempt to leave the room when I round the corner and meet the debris that Richard has just crawled through to get to me.

"Cole please listen to me the- I don't think so I am going to stay here and wait for Jane myself you can leave! Since you couldn't do It right yourself the first time, don't be mad at the manner I choose to fix what you and AJ broke!"

My skin is Fuming and the notion I am about to lose it has me second guess my proximity to Richard. *As much anger that I have towards him as I do. I don't want him hurt because of me.*

"*Richard, Leave now!*" My eyes begin to fade black making the room disappear as the anger is so wrapped up in me as I shout out and a bolt of energy flashes from my body releasing an uncontrollable blast with a near miss to Richard. The ceiling falls around him trapping him on the other side of a wall with no way out. Richard hollers and the room goes silent and my vision clears as the tension fades. *"I need to figure out how to use and control this or I am going to get myself or anyone in distance of me killed."*

Turning to head into the room where Jane and Jessica was before we disappeared to our own respectable corners. I open the door and what do I see? It's Jane standing at a ready stance like she is expecting to fight to the death. "*Where did you go? Are you okay?*" Trying to keep calm as to what happened just minutes ago thinking *I can't let her know about my plans yet. I need to catch her off guard if this is going to work.*

She stays quiet for the first few seconds as if she is trying to come up with a way to lie to me gently.

"*Jane?*" I repeat.

She opens her mouth hesitantly and replies *"Jessica sent me to some room and then I ended back up here."*

"*How long was I gone?*"

"*It only seemed like a few moments and it was all over.*"

I know she is lying! I thought, keeping it to myself to see where she was taking this. Her face says it all: she has never been one to hide her true feelings even when we first met that's why we got along so well. We just said what we felt and got it out and over with.

I am not going to give her the chance to kill me!

I feel my powers emerging within my skin like goosebumps on your arms when you get a chill. My eyes begin to go black and now I can hear Azreals voice repeating in my head *"You or her you choose who you are standing next to in the end."* I brace myself and get ready knowing this will have to be quick or she will return the attack.

She looks away and I take my chance and send a blast of dark light in her direction hitting her. Hurling her back into the bed where she had me chained to like a prisoner. The thoughts of the last twenty-four hours unraveling in my mind do nothing but fuel my anger towards the world. With every surge of anger I have, the tunnel and surrounding room shakes and the tunnel devours us like we are its last meal.

Jane scrambles around on the floor and I'm not quite sure what she is looking for but I send more blasts in her direction missing her at every turn. *There I see what she is reaching for. Some kind of box that I can't make out in this intermittent light.* She scrambles behind the bed and things go silent for a split second.

Then with a familiar chime the buzzing and dinging returns and the room begins to shake more than previously witnessed. Jane lifts up into the air as if she is being possessed as I stare at her unravel. *"Maybe this is it for her or Maybe this is what takes us both out."*

She spins at a rapid pace and then drops to her hands and knees out of sight from me. She belts out *"Cole stop, we need to figure out how we can both survive this, there has to be another way!"* Not waiting for her to get the better of me I send another charge of power her way and miss. Rubble exploded in every direction. She quickly returns fire and hits me, sending me up against the wall knocking the breath out of me.

Wiping the blood from my mouth I just respond with "*You lied to me just to have an upper hand, You are choosing you!*" The pain in my voice must be present because her face shifts from anger and defensive to sad and worried.

"I am still your sister, Cole!" Then she sends a charge of light at me as I am laying on the ground against the wall defenseless at that very moment.

Hitting me it sends a stunned charge through my body that burns a hole through my body sending an ash like substance into the air. She hits me again just this time I see her eyes go dark nothing like I have seen her do almost as if she isn't herself. Black blood-like substance oozes from the wound she just inflicted. Her skin sets fire and the glow is almost too much to stare at.

Turning my head to not see what is coming knowing it is my undoing I see a shadow in the opposite corner, it is Azrael. He is waiting in the wings like a vaulter to pick at me when I am dead. "*Fight back*" he whispers in my direction "*Fight back now I say*" My arm begins to glow where Azrael's hand print is scorched into my arm sending an uncontrolled belt of energy through my veins.

I stand returning and matching the energy Jane is giving when I blast a charge at her meeting in the middle as if our powers are feeding into each other. The bolt of energy is fighting for power over Jane's energy and she screams out in rage and it takes over mine. The power is so aggressive that the room explodes and everything goes silent in the dark.

BRYCE

The driver pulls up to the warehouse and unlocks the door. He doesn't even look in my direction in the mirror or chime in with what they expected of me. He just puts the car in park and waits as if he has nowhere to be. I grab the door handle and give it a tug, opening the door wide enough for me to see my surroundings as I step out. There are no guards at the entryway door like last time. The building seems abandoned with no lights shining through the windows on the bottom floor and the other floors seem to disappear into the night sky.

Wondering what is waiting for me on the other side of this door as I march up the steps. Everything seems too quiet, like an ambush of sorts. A grunt to get my attention comes from behind and it is the driver. I didn't even hear him say "*This way*" with his ominous posture. He shifted to the side waving his arm out toward the back of the building. "*What is back here, Demetri?*" he doesn't say a word like he is deaf of sorts or has selective hearing. "*Is this a trap*?" Still no answer. We come to a door as he takes the lead. I stall for a moment, being suspicious of this whole event.

He leans in and whispers, "*No one is here. Richard was the only one that was guarding your sister and Demetri was at home. He left just before arriving at the abandoned house to keep watch as ordered.*"

"*Why are you doing this?*" I ask in hopes of him responding. He does and tells me "*he has a sister of his own and he doesn't care for the kidnapping and torture of women. In his eyes, women and children are off limits and that is just something he stands by.*"

Giving my approval as I nod I reach out my hand to shake his to show my appreciation he takes mine and demands that *"I hurry, the hourly checks will begin in a while and when they find your sister missing they will get a hold of Demetri and he will come looking for her."*

Without hesitation, I turn to head into the door amongst the dark tunnels. "*Oh, and one more thing, you are looking for a small door at the bottom of a tunnel with a hatch that will open up into the room she is in.*"

Making haste, I head in and start my search. Unsure if the thug that just led me to my demise or not as I creep around looking for the one door that will lead to Kelcey.

I come to an opening at the bottom of a wall that is about two and a half feet by three feet wide, just like he described. The dim light in the tunnel has me searching for a way to open this secret doorway into Kelceys room and nothing. Out of anger and anxiety for time I shove the door, it opens with a clicking noise. I don't even have to ease inside guessing the noise of the door scared Kelcey so much so that she whimpers.

I whisper out for her to hear me, but not loud enough to alert anyone if they are, in fact, outside the main door.

"*Kelcey, it's me*" I pause in the crawl space for a second to see if I have the all clear and nothing makes a move in my direction, signaling that I do. *"Don't move in case they are watching on the security monitors. We are going to have to move fast, so we get out of here before shit hits the fan."*

Looking around, I see a table of weapons that they used to torture their victims. Finding a pair of shears to cut the zip ties to free her hands and feet from the chair she is in, I grab them and free her.

I notice the marks on her feet, guessing that they hurt her. I look at her face and pull the gag that is around her mouth and ask her, "*are you okay*?" Looking at her feet, they look like cigarette burns on the tops and bottom of her feet.

Kelcey says "*I tried to fight them and escape, but when I landed a punch at this Demetri guy, he ordered the goons to fix my attitude.*"

"*Can you walk" I ask her?* She nods and replies, "*yes but it will hurt like a Bitch but let's get the fuck out of this hellhole."* We go to scramble to the passage that brought me to her so that we can disappear as fast as possible. But as she is climbing into the tunnel, the door behind us swings open and a six foot burly man enters and narrows his eyes in on the two of us escaping.

I just Yell for Kelcey to "*go and get out of here that I will be behind her shortly"* shutting the door behind her. Forcing a barrier between us, I brace myself for impact when the man comes charging at me. With one quick pass, I just shove him and his head collides with the wall. Giving me the perfect opportunity to get to the table of torture devices arming myself. The man shuffled to his feet just as fast as I could get there. I grab the first thing in my hand and it is a wooden baton. I beat him with it when he wraps his arms around my waist, tackling me to the ground, causing us to scrap like prison inmates. He finds the sheers that I left on the floor when I freed Kelcey from the chair they held in her and holds them to my throat.

"*Where did she go?*" He demands in a loud scruff

"I will tell you over my dead body" he smirks as the rise of the corner of his mouth shifts upward on his face as if he is blood lusted and hasn't seen action in a while.

"*My pleasure,"* he growls and with a swift arm he raises his hand and positions himself to stab me with the shears when I hear a gun fire off a round. With my eyes squinted shut, thinking I was the one that was about to die, the man drops the shears next to me. Slinging my eyes wide open, a stain of red blood seeps through his white shirt, and he falls to the side of the floor. Gripping with both hands, he lays there, not making a sound as if he is living his life in a blink of an eye when you hear his last gasp for air and his chest quits rising and falling. I *wasn't the one to shoot him*. I look around for the culprit. I then see Kelcey in the passage opening, holding a gun. Still positioned in my direction, I quickly ran and pried the gun out of her tight grip. She is stunned and in shock. As soon as the gun is in my hand, tears fall from her eyes.

"*Kelsey*," taking her face in my hands, I get right in front of her and repeat, "*Kelcey, we need to go. Let's go. We need to move.*" Kelcey blinks and the shaking turns to adrenaline and we turn to hurry out this place.

We make it to the end of the passage and climb out of the door to the open air. Taking a moment to breathe, we take in a deep breath. Trying to catch our breath, I look around for a way to escape the grounds and get back to help Jane, but Kelcey grabs my hand and pulls me toward the wood line. Not to draw attention to us, I just follow her there. It is the car that took me to her. The driver rolls the window down and it is the same man that helped me rescue her. Kelcey jumps in and I quickly follow, making sure to not be seen.

JANE

Cole doesn't give me a chance and with him sitting on the ground, he forces a charge of light out at me and I countered just the same with my own charge of light. Our powers meet in the middle and force one another to take charge and consume one another's energy. It is almost as if the powers are too strong. They are consuming each other, causing a surge. Cole screams in anger and it causes the light to surge in his favor. Focused in on my current situation, I didn't immediately feel the blood ooze from my nose. The room shakes as Cole screams and that causes me to scream in response, causing a blinding light as an explosion erupts, causing the room to crumble.

Smoke and dust create a thick blanket over the top of us and I can't see where Cole went. Trying to move my body, realizing that I am trapped under a beam that fell from the ceiling and now has me pinned from the waist down. *"The force of the blast must have gotten Cole as well."*

"*Cole,*" I force out of my body as I listen for his response, but nothing, no sound, comes from the direction in which he was before the blast. "*Cole, say something!*" Flames reach us from the house. *My guess is Richard sat it on fire knowing that we were going to kill each other, anyway. Guess this is his way of making sure he finishes the job indefinitely and gets in Demetri's good graces.*

As I inhale, the smoke fills my lungs. A rage of anger fills my heart as I lay beneath the beam and rubble, thinking about my life and what the meaning of it all was. Laying there under the chaos, my mind wanders to when I was a child and life seemed so simple and full of happiness. I still remember the best times that I would come downstairs on the weekends and mom and dad would be in the kitchen with the music playing. All the while they were hand in hand dancing around the kitchen Island and playing the name that music tune. That is always something that I had wanted for myself in this life.

To find someone that wanted the rainy days sitting in the sunroom interlaced between each other's legs drinking our coffee and just enjoying the fact that life is, in fact, great. I would catch dad out of the corner of his eyes watching mom when she was reading her books, smiling at the faces that she made as if she were the characters in the novel she was reading. And of course when mom caught dad watching her, smiling at the thought she was playing a heroine or villain in a novel, she would blush and cover her face just to yell "*Stop*" in a playful and bashful moment. "*He would just respond that you are so beautiful. My sunshine.*"

Coughing as I am looking into the darkness of the disheveled room, the thought of dying alone in this place will haunt me till I no longer Breath. Tears fill my vision and force me to close them. Coughing harder this time, I taste the metallic residue in my mouth that I am at this point very familiar with. It lingers with every swallow that I attempt.

Laying there as I feel a heavy weight smashing down on me, I get tired. I just keep my eyes shut and try to remember more of the good memories. Like the family dinners, we would all get to the table and with no sounds or distractions, the world only existed in that room at that very moment. We would talk about the day's adventures that have started and ended in the kitchen. We would laugh at Dad's funny "*Dad*" jokes and listen to mom about the concerns to the shelter that she volunteered at. The good, bad and ugly were always an open door with us.

My breathing gets shallow, and my skin begins to burn as if I was on fire. Guess the flames from the fire have reached me. Aching from the burning, I see a vision of my parents as I squeeze my eyes shut. The moment of my first fight with my best friend when I was sitting on the floor on the side of my bed in my room and dad had come in and sat with me listening to every word I said without interrupting. He took his hand and placed it on mine and said with a deep sigh, "*You Are Enough*". I leaned in and just hugged him. That was all it ever took. Reassurance from the ones that always gave me their all, their whole heart. That is where I got my strengths.

Or the time when mom would make cookies and let me lick the spoon with dad on the other side. Eating them just as fast as they came out of the oven. They were both so equally important to me.

Octavia C. Penn

The house shakes and I hear a voice so faint and weak amongst the rubble that I almost can't make out what they are trying to say. "*I never had a chance*" It was Cole. He was still awake, barely by the sounds of it. I hear Cole holler. He is starting to burn alive, and I shake uncontrollably, using what energy and strength I have left to try and move the beam that is crushing me. But as I lift it, it slips and crushes me more. Blood spews from my mouth and a puddle of blood consumes the ground around me. A piece of iron rebar has pierced my stomach, and the pain begins to burn from the inside out now. Cole hollers out a name I have never heard before, as if he was having a terrible moment with someone else in the room. "*Azrael, you lied!*" The screaming continued on for a few minutes as I tried to hum and hold my ears to block out the sound. *This is it. I thought, I am next. This is all I amounted to. Where is Jessica in all this? There is no way she is sitting by and watching her children burn alive after she led us to this path of fate and demise we didn't choose for ourselves.*

"*Jessica!*" I shouted. "*This is not what I asked for, hell I didn't ask for any of this!*" The room burst into a bright light at first and then went black all together besides the flames that seemed to be right next to me and gaining ground

fast. My powers inside of me are wreaking havoc, like flickers of lightning in the middle of a horrible storm. The burning of my skin intensified, and just when I thought it was me on fire, I realized that it was my powers that had my skin feeling like it was burning. My heartbeat slows down, and it soon becomes the only sound I can hear, causing that to be the focus of my attention. Every beat slows with every exhale.

Flames have now reached me, and my hair begins to burn. The heat from the fire and my powers have me in so much pain, the room begins to fade. With one more big inhale, I let out a scream that could break glass, causing my powers to explode. "***COLE***!" That last surge causes the rest of the building to collapse.

Cole and Richard

Listening to the battle for the win on the other side of this wall is more than I can seem to bear. Being trapped, listening to all of the slamming and yelling, makes my heart stop as I hold my breath and wait for the next impact. The sadness I think about as I see Cole's and Jane's lives unravel this way makes me hate the person I was when we were younger. If time was on my side, I would change the past and not help AJ with the predicament he was in. I would tell Jessica that her daughter was, in fact, alive and turn AJ over to the mob so he could pay for just his crimes. Instead of involving an innocent child in his schemes that lead to this unforgivable decision. As we all fight to survive this scenario, I wonder *if I will make it out alive*. The thought of burning in this small space just inches away from the only family I have left is nerve-wracking to me because I also know that even though I can't get out, the flames are headed for all of us. *I deserve this.*

There we go. They are at it again. The walls and ceiling begin to give way this time. Now the chunks of stone and debris are large enough to kill someone the moment they land on top of them. *Hoping that the tunnel kills me before the fire would be the best outcome, burning to death is not on my top ways to die if I could help it. In this case beggars can't be choosers.*

Cole screams and the echoes of the commotion ringing in my ears as the area between both theirs and mine fall silent. The hair stands on its ends on my arms as goosebumps rise, giving me the eeriest feeling in the pit of my stomach. The silence is deafening, and I know my fate is now sealed. *With the life of my child gone and no family to call my own left on this earth, I am ready to give up.* I sit down on the nearest pile of debris and close my eyes. *Thinking I don't want to see the end nearing, if this is it.*

Close my eyes and a tear wells up and slides down my cheek as the images of my late wife and our last

Christmas together. We were all sitting in the living room and with Cole practically under the tree playing with the trains that he had gotten. We were sitting on the sofa, piled under the blankets, watching Mom's favorite movie. This memory of this moment brings happiness to my soul.

The Room burns hot, and the smoke is thick and choking me, making breathing nearly impossible. Fear sets in. I slid back against the wall, away from the flames as much as I could at this point. I tuck my knees up against me and wrap my arms around them tight, like someone was telling me it was going to be okay. The space that I am in is so hot from the flames that I feel like I am in the furnaces of a Crematorium.

I feel like I am melting.

My pants are melting and stick to my legs, the hair on my body singes and the smell of it is nauseating. The smell of burning flesh fills the air and the smoke in the small space is consuming the air in which I breathe. My arms are now turning to a charred black color that begins to crack and bleed. *Not much longer and I won't have to live through this agony any more.*

Maybe I will rejoin them in the next life? Hopeful wishing on my end knowing all the crimes and sins that I have committed, I am almost positive the ferryman will be headed south with my ass no questions asked.

My life flashes before my very eyes and all the good times seem to not out way the bad in this case. *My life was wasted on the very people I shouldn't have given a second of time for. While the ones I truly cared for suffered and got whatever was left of me. I was so selfish... This is what I deserve.*

The flames are now running its course as I try to come to terms with my fate, but as it burns my flesh, I can't stay quiet any longer. The sounds that exit my body as I scream are unbearable, even for me. Heightening my pain senses to the max until I become so weak, my breathing nearly stops and my muscles stiffen. The room begins to completely fade black. I just lay there and with my eyes closed I can feel the final tear fall from my eye and disintegrate at the same time.

I no longer feel a thing as I slip off without further pain.

Bryce

As we ride in this car in silence, absorbing the smells of the leather and the flicker of lights as we pass them, my thoughts race. *I have already put her in danger once. I won't risk it again*. Heading back to the house, I ask Kelcey "*to go to the police station and wait, but she insists on not leaving my side."*

"Bryce, I am not leaving your side. If it wasn't for you, they would still have me locked in that room. Not knowing what would happen if you or Jane didn't find the list of items that Demetri wanted."

"Kelcey, you saved me, remember, the gun."

The pause and searching face on Kelcey as she tries to figure out how to convince me to let her go is almost like I am looking at her as a small child, scared to be separated from a parent. "*If you come with me, you have to do whatever I ask and do it when I say! If I ask you to run, you don't stop till you find someone with a badge to help you. Now... Agree or we stop and I make Mr.Goon here drop you off at the police station and force you to stay.*"

"*Okay, she shrieks, I will do as I am told. Just don't leave me by myself.*" Her Eyes glazed over in the agony of all that she has seen and been through. *That monster let them burn her with cigarettes, and I was helpless to get her out before it could be prevented.*

We turn onto 62nd and Kennedy street coming to a slow stop in the middle of the pavement. Where the house should stand, it is now in a blaze of orange and red shades of flames. The shock and sheer terror in my face made Kelcey grab a hold of my arm like her life depended upon it, followed by a dramatic gasp. Most of the house has already burned down and crumbled to ashes just leaving the century old bricks left standing with a charred shadow dancing among the flames.

"Bryce, what is going on?"

The driver rolls the window down and says, *"It looks like the problem is taken care of. Would you like me to take you to your house now?"*

"What do you mean, the problem is taken care of?"

"They informed me when your sister went back in for you at the warehouse that Mr. Demetri made a pit stop by the house on his way home and made sure we burned the house down with the problems inside, along with it."

"I'll kill him. Stop the car now!"

I go to open the door and Kelcey squeezes my arm to stop me. She sighs, with a stressful tone to go along with the frightened look on her face.

"Bryce It's too late,"

Staring back at her. The thoughts of Jane being in that fire make me sick to my stomach. Quickly turning to hurl on the pavement, I lean over to cup my face to steady the movement of my heavy breathing. My skin becomes clammy and beads of sweat building up around my brow begin to run down my face.

What if she is still alive... What if there is a way I can get to her?

Octavia C. Penn

The moment passes where I feel like I can't breathe, but now I want to pass out. I faintly hear the fire trucks coming up the street. With the sirens in the background nearing and the goon that is driving says "*y'all want to get out or go with me but I can't be caught here when the city shows up.*" I pause for just a moment and then turn my head to give him my response and my entire surrounding traces till it reaches the point of where I am shooting hot beams of anger out of my eyes at him. Blinking quickly to focus on him and with a stern voice I ask *"Will you take her to my house and make sure she is safe? I will be here soon if you could just help me out a little bit longer."* Taking my phone out of my pocket, I snapped a picture of his face. *"For insurance,"* I fiercely growl.

"Bryce", before she could finish what she said, I told her, *"I just need a moment by myself to process what this means for me."* She nods in a cautious manner and releases my arm that she still had a hold of. Leaving an indent from her nails that were digging into my skin.

"*Do we have an agreement?*" The goon grunts and shakes his head in approval, turns, and sticks out his hand. *"My name is Jack. After today, I am done with this business. I have never in my life approved of the way this life affects others, but I have a sister that is special needs and it pays well. So if you need me, I will be there. This will be something she would approve of."* With a short pause he sighs *"She is all I have left after our parents passed."*

Taking his hand firmly in approval, I get out of the car, giving Kelcey a wink and send them on their way. As I watch them disappear with the lights fading into the distance and for the first time since arriving, I don't know what to do.

The first set of fire trucks arrives at the end of the street next to the house. Watching as men and women in yellow suits and jackets pile out of the cab of the truck, sling on oxygen tanks and masks, getting ready to see if there are any survivors. They almost look like fire ants when you pour water on their mound. Scurrying to fix what is damaged so they could move on to the next day like nothing had happened. It must have been at least forty-five minutes since the fire started and they had to make their way across town through the traffic and red lights. Imagining with the flames as high as they are, the inferno that is ablaze has burned through the foundation of the home and turned the tunnels beneath it into an oven. Not sure anything could survive that amount of heat and smoke. Standing on the outside looking in, *I hope that there is some closure to this saga and that wherever she is; she knows no matter what, I will not forget her.*

Walking to the opposite side of the street, I grab my phone out of my pocket to call Kelcey to check on her and I see I have a missed message from an unknown number. Pressing my finger to the biometric scanner, it opens up to the home screen. Hesitant as to what it says or who it is from, I press the icon to open it.

Message vaguely reads, *the envelope is in your desk, top drawer…* The sound of tires creeping across pavement forces me to turn around to a black car creeping up to me and coming to a slow stop. The black passenger window slides down and out of the shadows, a hand heavily rests itself on the window seal. I don't move other than place my hand in my back belt pocket to wrap my hand around the grip of the pistol that Kelsey killed that man with. *I am ready,* I think, while adjusting my hand to fire if need be at this person.

"Guess you don't approve of which manner I solved our problems?" Demetri leans forward to make himself seen and my skin boils. *"I told you and the two pain in my asses*

that if you didn't take care of it, I would." the corner of his lip raises to reveal an evil grin and comments, *"You're welcome."*

Without hesitation, I pull the pistol out of my jeans and put it to his head and pull the trigger, causing blood and matter to splatter all over the inside interior of the car. I drop the pistol inside the window on his lap with his twitching body and smile.

The only response I could fathom was

"Fuck you!"

Not The End

Tires squeal and the car makes a u-turn in the middle of the street, disappearing around the corner out of sight. The sound of the gun going off drew attention from some of the police standing nearby. Two of them head in my direction and I just stand there waiting for them to approach. With my hands out of my pocket and in the air, I just begin to recite my name and badge number. Going through all the semantics of how I am the Chief of Detectives and I was here for the same reason they are. But I left out the fact that I knew who was in the home and why before it caught on fire. I need the night to process this all in my head before I tell someone this sad and vindictive story. A story of family, lies and betrayal. Being

Octavia C. Penn

that I am in all of it means I won't be able to control the outcome of the article and the report. My emotions are all over the place with anger and sadness and the overwhelming urge for vengeance.

Reaching into my pocket to once more read the text from the mysterious number, I quickly call for a ride share. Standing alone on the curb watching the home that I left to save Kelcey and abandon Jane to her demise, I watch the night air fill with smoke. The smoke stacking against each other as it climbs like a stairway to nowhere my mind wanders to Jane's home lying in the bed holding each other before all shit hits the fan. Watching as the smoke rises and the ash and embers free fall as they float to the ground, time slows to a point of almost stopping. I was furious when she told me what those two assholes were up to. When I cooled down, I understood she had questions she needed answers to.

The sound of a car honking brought me out of my trance with an awkward smile on my face. Realizing I wanted the moment to never end, but it did. Before stepping into the car, I give the remains of the house one long last look goodbye.

Octavia C. Penn

We will always have that one special night. Your arms entwined in mine and your heart beating against mine in the same constant rhythm I knew we were meant to be. Just not in this lifetime, I guess. I'll see you in the next life. I will always find you.

Sliding into the back seat taking in a deep breath, I close my eyes and a tear falls down both cheeks as I hold my breath to control it. "*Goodbye Jane,*" I whisper to myself as I wipe my face, knowing tomorrow is going to be even worse. The idea that I now live in this world without you breathing the same air as I, is something I can't fathom. Car breaks hard, flinging my head forward suddenly brings my thoughts to a halt just as fast.

"*Really*?"

The driver responds with *"Sorry for that, but this asshole of a driver in front of us just sat through the green light with no brake lights."*

At this point, I don't care.

I just want to get to the office so that I can take care of whatever is in the envelope of my top drawer. I am exhausted so much so that I doze off in the back seat as my muscles relax and the motion of the car rocks me off to another place all together.

The ride must have been at least twenty minutes and the man says in an aggressive but civil manner "*We are here*."

I open my eyes and see the building standing tall against the dark sky, and the only thing giving off light is a small lantern glowing by the station entryway. I pay the man and thank him for the ride and apologize if I snored, and He smirks, then I get out. Stretching my arms upward into the sky, waking myself up. I notice a bright star shining alone. Something so simple and bright, causing merriment and wonder in this world, just like Jane. Knowing that in the morning I will have a report on my desk about the fire and the findings of the dwelling. I just told myself *to turn it off tonight*. I can't change what happened even though I would give my own life to change Janes. Tomorrow will be here in a matter of hours at this point. Staring back at the door, I head up the stairs leading to my office.

What am I going to find? Does this have anything to do with what I have been battling the past few days? Out of the elevator doors, I round the hallway and past Blake's desk to unlock my door to my office.

Octavia C. Penn

It is open?

Maybe Blake left it unlocked, thinking I was coming back later and just forgot to lock it on her way out. Shrugging my shoulder and giving it no more thought, I just walk in and to my desk.

The room is dark except for a corner lamp in the room by the sofa and bookcase. Blake says it makes my office look more at ease and welcoming instead of intimidating.

Sitting down in the chair, I go ahead and turn the computer on so that it can boot up while I look for this envelope. My eyes wander to the drawer, thinking *it would be a bomb or some type of trap that Demetri set before I offed him in his own car.*

Bet he'll never do that again. A slight grin of the thoughts of malice that I just committed makes me chuckle just a bit.

"Aha" I see a plain white envelope with the word *Open* on it. Turning it over and lifting the metal butterfly tabs, I notice the envelope has an object in it that is heavier than a piece of paper. Looking inside of it there is a photo, a folded paper and a key. The key is a gold, brass antique looking key. Shrugging, I lay it down and glance at the photo. It is an

ultrasound of a baby, perfectly shaped, looking like it is sleeping on the back. It says *My baby girl.* Not sure if it is what I think it is, I open the paper.

> *By now, I am sure you are wondering how this got here or who placed it here. This is the information you will need to take down them all when the need arises. I just want you to know that I am in a better place now and don't come looking for me. Anyway, let's get on with this, shall we? The contents that Demetri is looking for are in a safety security box hidden in the wine cellar floor under the third row of wine. What you are looking for will be a box of money and a full confession from AJ on what he did to Cole and I.*
>
> *That should justify enough cause to get a search warrant to raid the warehouse and bust them all. Please do me a favor and keep the money. Maybe do some good with some of it and maybe take a vacation after the week we have had.*
>
> *Now to get to the main reason for this letter, I just want you to know I will also see you in the next life and maybe do me another favor. Don't take too*

long making the first move; life is too short.

With love,

Jane

Folding the letter and placings it back into the envelope, I add the rest of the items back to it. The light flickers and for a split second I thought I saw a shadow in the corner. A slight breeze shifts the room's presence. I feel chills come over my body as if I could feel someone standing over me… The smell of Jane's perfume fills the room and then gone all in the same moment.

I smile, knowing she is right. She will be just fine and if this letter proves it, this won't be the last time I will see her. Standing up, I push the chair back under my desk and leave with my heart at ease for the moment. I grab the lock on the door handle and turn the lock to secure it, and close the door behind me. When I turn to leave, the light goes out for a quick second and back on again. There is now a shadow at the end of the hall, standing just in front of the elevator door. Frozen in my tracks, my blood begins to boil out of rage that this day can't get any worse when I draw my pistol and brace myself for some more mob shit when a voice shrieks.

"Bryce…" The voice is of a woman…

Octavia C. Penn

About The Author

I am a mother of two beautiful children and a wife to an amazing man that supports me through all of my crazy adventures. I was 18 when I joined the Army and then later Honorably Discharged. Having my oldest a year later and my youngest almost 3 years after the fact.

I am many things as a woman, but never in my mind did I believe I would also be an assault survivor, child abuse survivor and, to top it all off, a rape victim. Surviving all this is no feat and to be able to emotionally finish a book helps to get the frustrations out. Especially in a time where depression was taking control of my life at full speed. Survivors Depression is such a real problem and coping with it sometimes is a difficult task.

With the support of loving family and support of friends, you never have to be alone. Even in the darkest hours of the day or night when your mind goes there. Pick up a phone and call anyone. Life is already such a struggle, don't think you have to do it alone.

You are not a burden; you are worth every ounce of breath you breathe in someone else's world.

Octavia C. Penn

Until the Stars burn out, the moon will always rise and the sun will always set, go be a star- O.C. Penn

Octavia C. Penn

ALSO BY OCTAVIA C. PENN

Blind Lies–Spring 2024

Burned and Broken–Winter 2024

* For updates you can find them on

www.octaviacpennwrites.com

Dedication

To my loving husband Clinton who without a doubt has always supported my goals and aspirations. Without you I would not have the life we share now. Love you with all of my heart.

To my loving kids Kayden and Hunter, this is proof that hard work and dedication to yourself will win in the end.

Always love yourself no matter the cost.

Octavia C. Penn

Epigraph

I am not what happened to me,

I am what I choose to become.

-C.G. Jung

I may be burned and broken but I will rise from the ashes and scorch the Earth you once walked on.- O.C. Penn

Octavia C. Penn

Trigger Warnings

Abuse Death Murder Violence Blood Kidnapping
Assault Graphic Sex Sexual Abuse Sexual Trauma
Graphic Scenarios Torture Gun Violence Trafficking
Kink Harsh Language Implied Assault PTSD Gore
Parent Loss Forced Proximity of Family Deceit
Heartbreak

This Book Leaves off on a CLIFFHANGER

Cast Of Characters

Jane- Daughter of Jessica and A.J.

Bryce- Chief of Detectives and Love interest

Cole- Friend/Found Family to Jane

Richard- Adoptive Father of Cole and Mobster

Prudence- Adoptive Mother of Cole/ Deceased

A.J.- Father to Jane and Cole

Jessica- Mother to Jane and Cole / Original Phoenix

Sara- Richards Girlfriend / Victim

Erin- Janes Friend / EMT

Micheal- Archangel

Gabriel- Archangel / Protector of Portals

Azazel- Demon King / Runs City of Fallen

Azrael- Fallen Archangel of Death

Demetri- Kingpin for Greek Mob

Printed in the USA
CPSIA information can be obtained
at www.ICGtesting.com
JSHW050503031123
51410JS00001B/1